VILE

J.E. & M. KEEP

ISBN: 978-1-988619-17-0

DEDICATION

To our friends who didn't judge, readers of The Keep back when we were first starting out, and Darknest Fantasy Erotica who encouraged us to keep going.

CONTENTS

ACKNOWLEDGMENTS

J.E. & M. Keep recognize that erotica can be very personal, and that everyone has their limits on what they wish to read. Because of this, we provide content warnings for all our erotica so that you can avoid any **triggering material** – or find the story you most want to read. If you want your book spoiler free, please skip this section!

This particular story contains blow jobs, hand jobs, M/F sex, Virginity loss, and some taboo (dubious consent) sex scenes that are not intended to be erotic.

CHAPTER 1

It was too late to turn back, not that she wanted to. The 'wastes' of the valley spread out before her as she crested the ridge. It was a strange assortment of grey, green and reddish brown all nestled into a large u-shaped valley with a blue snake of a river that wound its way through. Alexandra couldn't see it all from her position, but what she could see was far more than her world had encompassed for the past decade.

The heavy pack upon her back was a burden of more than just its weight. The technical equipment inside it represented the best bargaining tool her people in the bunker had for food and supplies.

A last desperate act to get what they needed to survive.

It wasn't even a full twenty four hours since she set out, according to the device imbedded into her forearm. It lit up her skin to tell her the time of day, tracking her body signs and serving as a control for disease, illness and pregnancy.

Even after the day of excitement and travel, she could see the look upon Marim's face in her mind before she set out.

Before Dawn Earlier That Day

As handsome as ever, even with his smooth, fair complexion creased with worry, Marim turned from the door to the medical office after shutting it. "I wish it didn't have to be like this," he said, the concern for her plain on his face.

The two of them were the same height, which fit, for they'd been friends for as long as either could remember, nearly inseparable. But whereas she had little use for lessons and learning, he'd committed himself rather fully to becoming a nurse and hopefully someday a doctor.

He made up for any other shortcomings he had with enthusiasm and dedication, as he did in all things. Just as his unimpressive stature as a man was made up for by gorgeous good looks, and his thick, long mane of hair. Though he tied the golden mess back in a ponytail, he tended to leave some flowing about his shoulders. While those emerald eyes of his, so wide and pretty, seemed to almost glitter with suppressed tears at her having to leave.

"If only one of the last two search parties would've reported back in by now," he stammered, rubbing an arm. The nurses outfit he wore consisted of a high collared, short sleeved white tunic, and plain black pants that fit him rather snugly down to his boots. All in all he made what was otherwise a dull ensemble look good.

"You hafta take that equipment to the old colony site," he explained again for the fifth time. "With any luck you can trade for some supplies to bring back and seeds to start up the old greenhouse, and... and maybe we'll become self-sufficient again." It was a long shot, they both knew it, but with most of the occupants of the bunker sick or dead due to the contaminated food they thought would see them through another couple years, and every search party they sent out for supplies failing to return or bring back anything, it fell to her. Even Marim couldn't accompany her, because he was the only standing medical officer, despite being but nineteen.

Her own blonde hair was pulled back from her face, yet she'd resisted the tears that glistened in his eyes, and stood straight, her lips curved into a forced smile. "Look, you just need to get over this. I'll be back, I'll be fine. You know this, I know this, and when I return with my arms full of food and presents and whatever else they're going to throw my way, I'm going to make you pay for making me worry about leaving YOU here all by yourself."

Her jeans and t-shirt would have been so simple and plain on someone else, but she filled them out just right, her curvy body tightening and stretching the material so snugly across her chest and ass. "Just make sure no one else dies 'til I get back," she teased, though there was a pleading there. She didn't blame him for the deaths, of course, but with each one, things grew worse for the ones still living.

Marim's handsome face somehow managed a smile, as he always did for her, but he was definitely worried for her, and she could see beneath the veneer to that. "Be real careful," he warned, "and before you try tradin' the good stuff, hide it somewhere. You don't know if the colonists still up there are like us still. They might've been on hard times, and turned to desperate measures."

Stepping to her without delay, he put his arms about her, pulling her into an embrace. "Just get back, no matter what happens. We'll figure somethin' out," he said, though it was weak. Without some deal or scavenged goods to bring back, nobody would make it.

She kissed his cheek before brushing past him. She'd never been big on sappy goodbyes, or long drawn out and emotional scenes, so it was comforting in a way to feel her shoulders square under the heavy load of goods as she set out.

A secret smile came to her lips as real excitement shone through.

Before Dusk Later That Day

Alexandra had made a good pace that day despite the burden on her back. Her enthusiasm for the first bit of freedom from the underground prison that was the bunker fuelled her motions. However, as the sun crept towards the horizon and the shadows grew long over the valley, she knew her time was nearly up. She'd have to hide out somewhere that evening to rest.

On the bright side she saw two things: in the distance along the opposing edge of the valley were the large, circular white structures of what must be the old colony. It lay past the river and the grey and black ruins of the old pre-cataclysm city that her mother might have known the name of, but it was within sight, and that counted for a lot. It was a couple days journey away, by her rough reckoning.

Secondly, she could make out some building at the edge of the next ridge before coming into the valley proper itself. A long structure, it was at the end of a broken grey road, and she could make out no signs of life around it, and wouldn't even take her half an hour. She'd have noticed it sooner, but from her point higher up it was masked before now.

Alexandra had energy to spare, especially on such a big day, and as she set her sights on her evening destination, her red lips parted into a wide grin. She didn't let the fear of the unfamiliar edge into her consciousness, or the fact that so many disappeared into the unknowns. Instead she simply set out to rest for the night, her legs working to carry her over the last stretch.

She was so full of excitement for the journey ahead, and the entire world she'd never been able to explore that she never noticed the sounds ahead.

Approaching the long, rectangular building's side door, she was taken by surprise when it abruptly burst open. The metal frame struck her and sent her toppling away onto her side. She had little time to make sense of what happened next, stunned as she was, but three bodies came rushing out.

It was as those six hands grabbed at her that it started to come into view amidst the rough jostling. They were men, but they weren't like any men she'd known in all her days in the safety of the bunker.

Their faces were deathly pale, their features contorted into looks of pure rage. They wore little but shredded and damaged vestments of the past that covered their chests and loins, terrifying body paint about the rest. They screamed at her in violent rage as her senses snapped back.

CHAPTER 2

Her brown eyes went saucer wide as she tried to struggle away from them, shocked from the pleasant reverie she had been experiencing not seconds before. The suddenness of it all left her little time to think or understand, but she stated, quite loudly and firmly, "I'm sorry! I didn't know this place was taken!"

She heard no words from them, though they were far from silent. Their screams were manic, laced with pure hatred and venom. They did not seem like any normal people, and as she struggled to communicate with them they took her backpack from her and pinned her to the ground. In the shadow of the building, and the frenzy of the moment, it became hard to see what two of them were doing, the one atop her having her attention.

She had strapped a knife to her hip, but that was of little use to her in such a pinned state. She had seen nothing prior to coming down here, and she cursed herself, quite loudly, at having been less prepared. Still, as she stared at the man atop her, she was far from submissive. Her knees and elbows sought out the tender flesh of his body, probing for a weak point she could reach.

Time spent sparring in the bunker with Marim and her friends had left Alexandra strong and fit. With a swift kick of her knee she struck the savage man between his legs with such force she heard the very unpleasant sound of flesh crushing and caving in. With a hit of her hand to his head, he went sprawling off of her into the dirt suddenly silent.

There was no time for celebration though, for one of the others let loose a shrill cry and came at her, unbothered by his companion's fate as he bared his teeth and hard, jagged nails.

Her hand immediately went for the long, sharp hunting knife in the sheath on her hip. Her eyes were narrow as she stepped backwards. "Give me my shit back!" she demanded. She almost looked as crazy as he did, the way her body was half covered in dirt and her ponytail was matted with soil.

Screaming as he charged at her, the crazed savage made no intelligible response. For all his crazed vigour, however, she was a step ahead. Smoothly her athletic frame carried her out of his way, and he went crashing into the dirt next to his friend. Unlike him, however, he was back up again in no time and let loose with another blood curdling cry, only seeming more incensed by her frustrating him.

She was of average height, but she was spry and adrenaline pumped through her. Though she had walked all day with the pack on her back and was previously weary, the lack of the weight and the excitement of danger charged through her. As she tried to keep her distance, she kept slashing at the air with practiced swipes designed to keep an enemy away.

The grace and confidence with which she moved in the face of such freakish horror would've been enough to cow most attackers. The slashing hunting knife kept him at bay, though didn't hit.

Uncut thus far, the savage man took advantage of her missed slash and charged in again. This time he had her, and the impact of his blow knocked her back into the ground. The pale lunatic let loose some cry of mixed rage and victory.

It was in that moment, however, that–almost simultaneously–a shot rang out, echoing across the hills, and the man's head exploded on one side into a mist of red. It was the goriest sight of her life, but it was accompanied by the visage of that madman toppling over to his left away from her, lifeless.

In the opposite direction she immediately traced its source. She could see, silhouetted against the setting sun, the outline of a tall man. Standing still with a rifle at his shoulder, he wore a long trench coat with a wide brim hat on. Only her keen sight and fast reflexes allowed her to see much of anything of him, for the glare of red, setting sunlight hid him almost entirely.

"Oh, ew," she moaned as she shuffled away from the dead man, her grip tightening on her blade as she looked towards her saviour. "There's another one! If you wanted to keep being helpful, I mean!" she practically begged as she looked towards the area she had last seen the thief. She tried to avoid the messy pile bleeding on the ground, but a morbid fascination kept bringing her gaze back to it.

There was no sign of the third man, nor her backpack and gun, and the way her saviour shouldered his rifle and began to saunter in her direction showed he was in no rush to go chasing after anything.

It took longer than it should've to make out the man's features due to the glare of the sun behind him. Instead, the first personal bit of him she experienced was his voice, rich and smooth, "I didn't see a third," he stated, then called out over his other shoulder, "did you see a third Bren?"

From off to the side she saw a large man, about as tall as this first one, but much, much broader. His voice was deep and baritone, "Nah boss," and he too carried a gun in his hands. She could see his dark hair and pale features as his direction kept the sun on him, instead of behind him. With a short, trimmed black beard, he was a large bear of a man in a beaten old leather padded vast and worn pants.

After the adrenaline rush she just experienced, she was practically hopping from leg to leg, "What, you think I'm lying? Fuck, I'll go get my shit back, then. Thanks for that one," she offered, her eyes opening wide, as if daring them to let her go alone. She was so cocky she even started moving towards the door, her sneakers leaving dirty imprints behind as her t-shirt rolled up over her holster, exposing a sensitive sliver of the low of her back.

The two men didn't move after her immediately. Instead they paused and looked at one another in some silent communication.

By herself, she headed on in cautiously. Luckily for her, the rectangular building's windows were all facing the sunset, and its light poured in illuminating the ancient building; rows upon rows of old worn, slashed and punctured seats, by battered or toppled tables. She saw no movement, nor any real sign of habitation.

She didn't hear the man's approach until he spoke, that smooth, masculine voice without a face, "I don't know what you think you're lookin' for," he said, "but those fuckers don't run and hide, miss." Having caught her off guard she looked back and finally saw him.

His hat was off now, and long, pale-blonde–almost white–, straight hair spilled down around his ears before going down his back. His face, however, was a contrasting darkness, smooth and unblemished but for a single scar at the left side of his jaw. He peered down at her intensely with dark brown eyes.

Her face was contorted in anger as she spun to look up at him, "Well he fuckin' took my bag and my gun, so either it was a ghost or they do run and hide," she barked. Her eyes were slightly watery and she brushed her fingers against her lashes as she started moving in deeper through the building. "A bag of shit doesn't just get up and walk off my back."

The larger man, Bren, backed into the old diner, gun at the ready, obviously watching their rears. The tall slender man, however, followed along quietly, his gun ready but otherwise not seeming too alarmed despite the circumstances.

There were a couple doors leading from the long, main room, but one was barred by trash that hadn't looked disturbed in quite some time. Heading through the other door, however, she kept on the lookout, gun at the ready. Alexandra and the slender man made no noise as they advanced, him treading silently behind.

When the attack came, it took her by surprise once more. A scrawny, pale woman lunged out with a piercing scream, though before she could hit either one of them, the tall man struck out, the hard butt of his gun striking into her face with a loud crunch of cartilage, sending the attacker back into the closet she'd pounced out of into a heap.

"Ulg!" Alexandra stumbled just from the shock, before she straightened herself. "Fuck, that's not him," her eyes moved around what she could see of the thief or her bag, before finally resting her sight upon the man towering over her, "You been 'round here long? Where would they go if they all of a sudden decided they wanted to hide?"

Having encountered more trouble, the tall, handsome man slipped past her, and she could see he moved—even in his bulky trench coat and large boots—

with a rather generous helping of grace and aptitude. Moving ahead of her he went by the door at the end of the hallway. It was barred over–nailed shut in fact, though the work looking done many years prior–then took the only accessible door, pushing it open and peering in cautiously.

"Nothin'," he said at last, and then stepped on in. The room was mostly filled with metal fixtures, obviously a kitchen, though there seemed nowhere a man–let alone a man with a large pack–might hide inside.

"Okay, so... this is weird, right?" she frowned, her adrenaline having spiked, leaving her body slightly slumped. "I mean, I had my bag, that guy took it, then those two psychos attacked me. Now he's disappeared?"

Stepping back towards her, his cautiousness seemed to slip away again and he was casual, she could even note the sound of broken glass crunching beneath his boots as he approached her. "Like I said, they don't run and hide," he took his rifle and brought the hoop back up over his shoulder, letting his dark hazel eyes roam up and down her form. "And I never heard of 'em stealin' before either. Unless it was a person or meat, that is."

"Well, there's a first for everything, I guess. And now I'm just fucked. Great," she slammed her back against the wall, her pale skin flushing an angry red under her light hair. "Fuck, fuck, FUCK," she brought her ponytail to the wall again and again as she threw her tantrum.

With an arched brow the dark, ruddy skinned man watched her with some curious interest. Bren came in, the sounds apparently alarming him for he had his stubby rifle at the ready, though the 'boss', as he was called, held out a hand, assuring him it was okay. The dark haired Bren gave her an obvious once over then left, leaving the two of them alone again.

"Could'a lost a lot more," was what he said at last. "Most folk know better than to fight back and raise their ire." A smirk took his face, and though it'd look smug on most, he managed to make it appear appealing, "But you took that one fucker out faster than I've seen Bren drop a man."

"Asshole had it coming," she scowled, though there was a twinge of pride in both her words and her expression. "Woulda got the other one, but glad I didn't have to. Still. Now I'm fucked, so it doesn't matter. Nearly got killed for nothing."

With a shrug of his shoulder, that might've been to readjust the rifle over his back, or in dismissal of her words he said. "Startin' over's something we all get used to out here," and he looked her over again, then once more, as if seeing her for the first time. "You look pretty damn good to be wandering alone." Crossing his arms over his chest he asked, "You an escaped van-girl?" he asked.

"What?" her face contorted in obvious confusion, as if trying to figure out what any of that meant. "Look, if I don't get my bag back, a lot of people are going to die," she sighed, exasperated, "So can you help me look through this place?"

Recoiling just a bit at her claim, the man grinned, apparently finding some humour in the situation she did not. "People gonna die," he said as if her words were comical. "Heard that one before," chuckling he gestured around and said, "Look sugar, there ain't much to look around in here, as you've seen. And though you may have people that might die if you don't get your package of life-savers, I actually got people whose lives I need ta look out for."

"Well then thanks," she bit back acerbically at him, starting to move into the corner of the room, intending to search every corner of it for a trap entrance or secret door. Her hands moved across the flooring and walls, knocking on it before moving a few steps and repeating the process. She kept her knife ever ready in one hand, her eyes constantly moving around the room as though being hunted.

The tall man watched her a while, as if he'd not seen anything so entertaining in a very long time. It wasn't until she'd searched half the room with her meticulous care that he spoke up again, "Hey hun," he began, "what's your name anyhow?" he had his head tilted, and at some point must've ran his hand through his hair, for it looked thicker and better now, and the strange—definitely bleached–blonde look of it was surprisingly appealing on his dark features.

"Alexandra," she responded, her own blonde hair lacking its usual bounce, the long waves piling down around her shoulder and over her simple cotton t-shirt. Her black jacket was very light and more of a protection against the elements than the cold, and she left it unbuttoned, ending about half way down her back. "Don't you have lives to save?"

She was a treat for the eyes, to be sure, and his were feasting on her. "The name's Jarago," he said, the sound rolling off his tongue so naturally, he made it sound as if it were a delicious snack. "And as for lives ta save, well," he shrugged his shoulders again pulling back his trench coat and stuffing his hands in his pockets. Beneath that heavy coat, he wore a simple vest and black pants, lined with buckles and straps. He looked like a handsome actor done up in the gear of a hard-nosed traveller from a movie. "I could make you an offer. Seein' as how you're shit out of luck, and shit out of... everythin', it seems."

"What kind of offer?" she asked, still repeating the tapping motions, but she was remaining more and more focused on him, her voice becoming just a bit more hopeful. Happiness and joy befit her face well, though he was only starting to see the faintest traces of it beneath the surface of her panic and fear.

Jarago leaned back against what once must have been a clean counter, but now was encrusted with rust and a film of grime. "My crew is gonna set up camp here for the night before makin' our way onwards." Pulling back his collar a bit he sized her up, "That'll give ya a night to search, and if in the mornin' ya ain't found yer bag of life-savers, I'll offer ya a position. Could use a gal like you," he said, a wry smile forming on his face as the look he gave her suggested more than his words alone.

She stared at him blankly, but the slight colour that rose to her cheeks spoke to her awareness of what he was saying. "Fine, yea, alright. Wait, how many of you are there?"

Holding up a hand he flashed her four fingers, "Four all told. Bren and me, then the other two, they're hired hands. Me and Bren though? We're tight," he said with all seriousness, pushing away from the counter and making his way slowly towards the door, "We'll be settin' up for the night like I said. Call out if you find any more of 'em hidin' in a cabinet," he said with a smile, though somehow he managed to make the expression look less condescending than his words made it sound.

"I'm sure you'll hear me - or him - scream. Promise," she said, going back to her tedious work. She was prepared to hunt every inch of this shithole, because there was no way she was returning back to the bunker just to tell everyone she lost all the goods before the sun even set on the first day. She was not going to deliver them into death.

CHAPTER 3

After a couple hours of fruitless search through the decrepit wastes of old humanity, the sounds of laughter and the smells of cooking food arose. Coming out, she saw sat around the fire the large man Bren, and Jarago, with another unidentified man in the corner seeming to sleep. They were being pretty noisy really, but it seemed the man in the corner was used to it and didn't budge.

Turning towards her Jarago bore a big grin, and Bren gave her a stoic but intense look. "Well, look who it is Bren, our little fire-cracker. Y'know," he said, shooting a mock serious look to the other man, "I don't think I should poke fun, judgin' by how fast she can down one of those fuckers, it just ain't smart."

"I'd say you're right," she agreed, plunking down on the floor beside him. "Besides, I'm a lot more pissed off now than I was then," she drew her legs out, stretching them and her back for a moment. "I have no idea where that asshole went."

With a plastic bowl for a dish, Jarago forked something in it that smelled like meat and popped it into his mouth, eating. "Don't know what to tell you about that," he said seriously, "it ain't in their nature to run and hide." With a shrug he said, no longer mocking, "If one of 'em had your stuff and then was gone, he's either on his way to do somethin' horrible with it, or he'll be back for you."

"Think he belonged to New Atlantia?" she asked, looking at Jarago intently. Her stomach growled, but she rubbed her arms over it to silence it quickly. "Fuck, if he's off trading it... Might be better going back," she sighed, curling her legs up and resting her chin on her knees, staring at the fire. She was so lost in her own thoughts she barely showed any interest in the men or who they were, which was so unlike her usual, curious self. While she never cared much for learning, she loved learning about people, watching and talking to them. Especially as these were the first people she'd really met out in the wastes.

It finally dawned on her just how out of sorts she was behaving, and stared back at Jarago, "Why are you here?"

She had been so lost in her own reverie she failed to notice the bewildered looks the two men were giving her. They obviously didn't understand a lot of what she said, though Jarago answered, "We're a caravan, Alex," then cleared his throat.

Laying down his tray he said, with furrowed brow, "Just where are you from? And where are you headed anyhow?" Bren looked almost equally as confused, though his stoic face hid it better as he sat, arms crossed.

"One of the bunkers," she said, her head tilting to the side. It was obvious that there was something lost in translation between them, and she slowly moved her legs to sit more comfortably. "And I'm going... was going... to New Atlantia to get some supplies. But now I don't have anything to trade."

This time it was Bren who was first to look to her and speak, "That explains a lot, Boss."

Jarago nodded, wiping his hands on his pants as he sized up the beautiful young woman anew. "A bunker babe?" he said, a smile returning to his face. "And you were headed to... New Atlantia?" He sounded as if the name was a bit unfamiliar to him, then pointed off out the broken windows of the dilapidated restaurant, "The big white place... over there? Other end of the valley?" he asked.

"Van girl, bunker babe, what next?" she sighed, though her eyes twinkled with good humour. "And yea. Why, what do you call it?"

"Hell," answered Bren immediately, the large, stoic man quick to respond once more, a hard look on his broad face.

Jarago nodded to that, "Damn straight," he affirmed. "And those pieces of shit that attacked you aren't gonna trade anythin'," he said with certainty. "Oh, it came from Hell–New Atlantia–alright. Or very likely anyhow," he said with a shrug, "but ain't no

PERSON who goes there and ever comes out right again," he said sternly. "That's where you go to die, or have every bit of your humanity stripped from you. Either way, you might as well be dead."

All the while Bren nodded authoritatively to Jarago's words, his jaw set firmly as if he was put on guard just by the mere topic.

Her brows furrowed and they could see her breathing begin to rise. As her posture straightened further, her hands resting at her sides, she looked to Bren, "Why would they steal my tech stuff?" she asked curiously.

The two men gave her that strange look again, as if she were mad. With a deep intake of breath and a shake of his head he said, "Like I said, the Viles don't go runnin' and hiding, and they don't steal. Unless it's to steal a person or some meat–they like eatin' meat." He shrugged his shoulders, "Just not how they do things, sugar. Never has been."

"Yea, well, that doesn't change what just happened. Fuck, why would I even make this up?" she asked, frustration creeping into her voice as her fingers went to her hair, finally trying to get the dirt free of the thick waves. "They took my stuff, I don't know why and you say they wouldn't have."

The two men glanced at each other for a moment then Jarago looked back to her, "It's not that we don't believe you, it's just that... it doesn't make any sense by our accounting," he said. With a jerk of his chin the tall, darker man gestured for Bren to go, "You take watch for now," he said.

Bren got up, picking up his own rifle and looking over the woman, a glint of curiosity, disbelief and more yet on his face, then turned and left, leaving the two alone with the sleeping man.

Her fingers ran through the long, blonde hair before she finally gave up trying to fix it, staring up at him with an annoyed expression, "I've just pretty much killed everyone I've known for the past decade, and it's sure as hell more than three people in a caravan. How's that for having to start fresh."

Arching a brow over at her, the tall Jarago lifted himself on one palm and slid over next to her, speaking lower. "You've got a pretty grim outlook," he said, "like I told ya, folks out here–in the light–are used to havin' to start from nothin'. And you're fortunate, you already got a job offer," he explained, a wry, handsome smile lighting his ruddy-brown features. "Work for me, I'll see you treated well, and in time you'll earn some extra to help your friends."

She met his eyes, not flinching away, "Yea, about that. What exactly did you want me to be doing? Killing those things full time or just being your adorable little bunker babe plaything, huh? 'cause I'm not sure either of those really flies with me."

His smile widened to a smirk and he put up his two hands, "Why not both?" he said. "You got the tenacity for one, and the looks for the other," he said, reaching a hand out, touching his fingers to her knee. "We can come to an arrangement," he said softly. "Not like you'd have to put out to everyone like most van-girls do. I'd keep you to myself. Maybe Bren now and then. If you're up for it," he offered.

Her eyes went down to her knee, studying the strong hand before looking back to him, a mixture of unreadable expressions on her face. "Okay, firstly, what the fuck is a van girl? Secondly, how long would it take for me to get some seeds and food for a colony of dying people?"

Looking only mildly surprised by her statements he gave a light shrug, but left his hand on her knee. "I don't trade in that sorta stuff," he explained, "but in time along our routes we'd come across the sort of materials you're lookin' for, I'm sure." Clearing his throat he added, "And a van-girl is a woman who tags along on a caravan to see to the needs of the caravaneers. I mean, alternatively there's van-boys too, of course," he explained.

Her lips pursed to the side as she pressed her hands into the dirt, seeming thoughtful. "What type of stuff do you guys do, then?" she asked.

The man's strong hand lingered on her, then slowly began to stroke against her thigh, him leaning towards her rather familiarly, "Weapons," he explained. "Scavenged goods too. We deal in hardware," he said, stressing the 'hard' just a bit.

"God, has it been a while for you or something?" she tugged her thigh away from him, though she didn't seem upset. "What would I have to do, and how would I get the stuff I need then, huh?"

He didn't seem to appreciate her sharp disapproval, though he smoothly took his hand back and placed it on his own knee. "You'd have to keep me happy," was his firm response, "Bren too, now and then, but mostly me. And you'd get what you need by doin' your job well, like everyone else. When we arrive at town, you'd get a cut of the profits that you could use to buy the shit you need."

Her gaze turned back to the fire, and she stared deep into its pits for what seemed like the longest time but was only a half-minute or so. A big breath rose her chest and she let it out before staring at him again, "And how hard are you to keep happy, hm?"

With a light shrug of his shoulders he gave her a look over, "Lookin' as you do, won't be difficult I don't think." Testing his luck again he brought his hand back over to her, laying it directly upon her thigh this time as he spoke quietly near her ear. "You're a real good lookin' gal, and I ain't half bad myself," he said with a confident grin, "I'll make it fun for us both even. And you come along for the ride, paid and no worries."

"And I can leave whenever I want, right?" she still spoke with such confident determination, even as she appeared to be capitulating to him. "And you and your... caravan won't hurt me," she added on.

With a bit of a laugh he nodded, smiling unevenly, "Yeah, that's right. Leave whenever you like, as long as you keep me happy in the mean time– and I mean *real* happy–and none of us'll harm you, I can guaran-damn-tee that," he said, his fingers probing along her inner thigh again brazenly as he lofted a brow and gave her a querying look.

Despite her calm exterior, she felt her heart beat begin to pick up in her chest and her breathing grow more shallow, despite her best attempts to keep it well paced. Looking back to the fire, her lips were parted and her face conflicted. Still, a thread of excitement was being tugged through her, that same familiar feeling that she had when she first left the bunker. That feeling of adventure and risk, of things new and unknown.

When she looked back at him, her eyes danced with her hidden desires, and she gave a nod of her head, "Subject to revision, I currently agree to your terms."

His smirk widened further still to full-fledged grin, and he gave her thigh a squeeze. With a shrug over his shoulder he indicated back to the hallway towards the kitchen she'd searched so thoroughly earlier, "C'mon then." He was getting up almost as soon as he said it.

CHAPTER 4

She was a bit slower, though that wasn't saying much, and she dusted off her behind as she walked. A tentative glance was given to the sleeping travellers, but there was something much more demanding on her mind, and her steps quickened to keep up.

As far as losing one's virginity went, it surely wasn't ideal. But then, no ideal situation had ever popped up, not with how much everyone gossiped in the bunker. Even Marim couldn't be trusted with her virginity, though the brief thought brought a pang of regret. She probably would have slept with him after she found out she was leaving, if it didn't feel like it was going to be an emotional event.

Alexandra didn't really sign on for that type of thing.

Stranded out there in the wastes of the old civilization, following after a handsome stranger, it was her best option. Especially if he was going to be her ticket to get to safety. She further justified to herself, she would be saving lives as she did; she certainly couldn't say she had an opportunity to do that before.

Jarago had moved so silently and quickly, he was already in the old kitchen, throwing his trench coat over top of one of the less filthy tables, leaving it spread out as sort of a blanket. She could see him now a bit better, even in the dim light of the room, lit only by the small windup lamp he'd brought. The vest he wore was apparently padded with some protection, and he wore nothing on beneath, showing off his dark muscled arms. It was obvious he didn't sit back on his missions doing nothing.

Brushing his long, straight hair back, he undid the vest and leaned against the table, watching her. "Fresh from the bunker, huh?" he asked, "When'd you leave?" His voice was quiet, not carrying beyond the room with the two of them.

"This morning," she moved towards him, standing just inches away with her arms folded under her breasts as she looked up at his face, the shadows dancing across both of them, flattering them both. Not that she needed flattering lighting to be attractive. Her features were beautiful and clear of blemishes and scars, and despite the mess of her long, wavy pony tail, she was still above most any he'd seen.

With the ample swell of her breasts and rear, it was hard not to understand why he'd taken an interest.

With his vest undone he pulled it up over his head then tossed it to the floor beside them carefully. His body beneath was lean and well sculpted, his skin a smooth, even colour all across, showing his dark flesh was definitely not the result of a tan. Reaching out he placed his hands on her hips and pulled her in against him as he looked down.

"That fresh out of the bunker, huh?" He said, lifting his lips and shaking his head in some disbelief. "Been years since I heard of someone climbing out of one of those things," he gave a light laugh, leaning down just a bit. "Been about a decade myself since I came out," he added, so close to her now, letting her see the fullness of his smoothly chiselled good looks, lined by the shadows cast with his lamp.

Her fingertips danced lightly against his chest, exploring the flesh and the muscles beneath, trailing her nails teasingly along his body. "You musta seen it all, huh?" she asked, her eyes staring at his chest, transfixed. She took in a deep breath as her stomach turned, excitement and anxiety brightened her features and pushed away the dull sleepiness that threatened her. Did she really want to go through with this?

So daring and never showing a moment's hesitation, his hands slid up from her hips over her stomach, brushing against her breasts before he pushed back her coat from her shoulders, sliding it off so smoothly. "Just about," he said, tossing her jacket atop his vest on the floor. "Don't get to be a caravan man for this long without seein' and doin' a whole hell of a lot, Alex."

"And yet you've never seen someone steal a backpack," she tutted, her fingers going back to his body and creeping lower along his abs, finding that treasure trail and gliding down it. Her fingers were so soft and smooth, saved from hard, manual labour and difficult living for most of her life. Her skin was so light in contrast to his, and she enjoyed the scene ahead of her, even if she was scared.

He sported a glorious male physique, abs so hard and firm, that little trail of hair so pleasantly soft. Licking along his lips he gave a soft laugh, "Seen plenty of stealin', sugar." He rubbed her shoulders then moved back down, brushing once more against her large breasts before coming to her waist, fingers curling in under her shirt, "Never seen a Vile do it though."

"It was a human," she said, a little confused even as her hands rose up, allowing him to strip her of the light, cotton t-shirt and exposing the white lace bra beneath. It hoisted her breasts, the shadows delving between the thick cleavage, skirting just above her nipples. Her stomach was smooth and flat, though not to the extent of being toned.

Adding the garment to the growing pile, his hard, but smooth fingers stroked over her stomach, and up along to the sides of her breasts, cupping and squeezing them through her bra, the tips of his digits pressed into her breasts. "No hun," he said, "they ain't humans anymore," and despite the grim topic, she could feel his manhood respond to her through his thick black pants. "They're what becomes of a human after that shit they pumped into us ten years ago goes wrong," he explained.

She clearly didn't get it, but her fingers worked against the button of his pants regardless, "Well maybe if they don't steal, then the thief was fine." Her palm moved down, over his clothed cock and rubbed against him, even as she worked the zipper down. The feel of it through his clothes delighted her, that heavy, firm bulge pressing into her hand, so constrained and delightful. The familiar motions brought back pleasant memories of illicit rendezvous with so many different faces, all so enjoyable in their own way.

Even though she'd never had sex, she was amazing at doing everything but. After all, she'd spent years practicing. As her eyes turned up to his, her lips curled into a smile.

Still swelling to his full size, the man was surprisingly big. She could feel the heat of that large organ pressing against her palm, and knew by the time it was done growing it'd be a hefty cock to blow away the ones she'd jerked off and sucked in the bunker.

For his part, his hands slipped around to her back and deftly undid the bra, "They don't work with anyone but other Viles, and the Passives they enslave," he said, tossing the garment away. Even as she pulled free his organ, the thick, well curved shaft so thick and heavy, he said, "There's the Viles, who went nuts and kill, the Passives, who do whatever anyone tells 'em, then... there's us," he said, cupping her tits.

She was so heavy in his hands, that perfect curve and weight, the pink little nipples topping the breasts, still so perky from youth, despite their size. She shifted even nearer to him as she began to stroke him, and he could feel her body warm against his, both literally and figuratively. A heat ran under her skin and she seemed so much more at ease and relaxed than just moments prior. Her grip was firm and steady, and her brown eyes stayed on his, "Let me know what you like."

He gave an approving little groan as her hand began to pump his cock so expertly. It was obvious she had experience; women didn't usually know how to jack a man off well, but this one...

Feeling out her heavy tit flesh, his own hands coaxed such pleasant feelings from them, teasing her pink little nipples as he leaned in and gave her neck a kiss beneath her ear. "Drop the pants and bend over the table," he commanded quietly, his cock already oozing precum onto her fingers as she pumped him. It'd been a long time for him, she was right.

It wasn't how she expected her first time, but then, she wouldn't have expected the order to bring such a burning hot delight to her body. Despite her feisty nature, it brought something out in her that seemed only too excited to emerge, and even though she never let him go as her fingers worked her own button and zipper, pulling down her jeans and her panties rather unceremoniously, she moved into position.

She could feel her body tense and release, excitement spilling through her as she wondered if it would hurt. If it would feel good. If this was what she wanted. Reluctantly she let his cock fall from her adept hand as she braced both arms on the table, her breasts pressing into the protective jacket beneath.

His own pants undone and tugged down just past his hips, the neatly trimmed patch of light hair above his magnificent and large cock was on display. He slipped around her, his hands never leaving her flesh, feeling out her smooth, perfectly unblemished skin along to her hips and ass.

She felt his heated cock brush against an ass cheek, but then something changed. Instead of him lining up to plunge in, he bent his knees and she felt his hands pry her cheeks apart. The next feeling was of his moist tongue lapping along her slit, the tall, dark man giving a little moan of delight at her clean, feminine taste as he teased her clit.

She gasped as she felt his wet muscle working against her, and her entire body flushed warm with the sensation. She couldn't suppress the loud moan, and she pushed herself up on tiptoes to allow him a more comfortable position.

"Aw fuck," she murmured, her head dipping low as her fingers grasped onto the jacket, the strain turning her knuckles white. Her body burned with her own desire, the wrongness of the situation and the stress of the day. She felt so worked up, and as he lashed her sweet nub, she could feel it rock her right to the core.

As much as he seemed quite adept at pleasuring her with his tongue, there was something about the way he moaned and licked at her so vigorously that seemed to hint he was just enjoying himself. Immensely.

The whipping lashes of his tongue coaxed her own fires up high, but they didn't go on forever. The well-hung man rose back up to his full height behind her, dick in hand, as he kept her cheeks spread. Nudging the bulging crown against her virginal slit, he spoke to her with his smooth voice a bit gruffer than before, "Love the smell of a nice, ripe cunt."

She cried out in frustration, feeling so close to the brink yet so far away, and she glanced over her shoulder at him as if to plead before she felt the thick, smooth head rub against her. All sense was lost as her legs parted, her toes pushing her up higher, her torso pressing against the table. She felt weak, and tired, yet the excitement he'd awoken in her would not rest.

"Be gentle," she managed out, sucking in a breath and smelling the scent of their sex commingling in the air.

Jarago gave a wry smile to her plea, but nodded, "Alright," he said. She could tell he was surprised by her request, though only seemed willing to give her what she wanted.

When the entry came it was, as he'd just promised, gentle. The bulbous, well-shaped crown of his impressive cock pressed plushly against her petals, parting them as he lodged himself inside just barely. Placing his two hands upon her hips, he gave a bit of a push more, only placing an inch or two of his length within but groaning from the slick squeeze, "Don't be afraid," he urged smoothly.

She was so wet, yet so tight. His cunninglingus had helped warm her to the experience, though, and at his words she felt her body obey, the tension leaving her shoulders and back as her breathing became more constrained.

It didn't hurt, not really. It felt strange and wonderful, but it didn't hurt. Her legs trembled as they struggled to keep her aloft, and she tried to part them further, finding the jeans to be holding her locked in place.

Over six feet high, he bent over her as he slid his length deeper into her quim. True to his word, he was gentle, though as tight and untrodden as her cunt was, and as thick as his girth got with each throb of desire, it was still not exactly an easy entry.

With his fingers dug into her ass and hips, he groaned a little as he lodged himself to her depths, snugly pressed to the very limits of her sex. "Damn," he cursed, his dick swelling with repressed desire. "I think I might even believe this is your first time," he said in a breathy voice, laced with longing.

"Yea," she breathed, her head dipping down as she felt his thickness throb within her. It was such a full, strange feeling, yet so pleasant at the same time. He was warm, and the sensation was almost comforting. She could feel his thighs lined up against hers, his hips pressing into the round curve of her ass, and she squirmed against him.

Shallow breaths and little sighs escaped from her as she felt so alive. So terrifically alive. Every sensation seemed more real, more tangible, more pleasurable, and she pushed back against him.

He didn't start on her right away, instead he bent down over her, curling his arms in under hers and kissed her shoulder blade, her spine, nuzzling her skin and hair as his cock twitched and throbbed inside her so eagerly. "You sold it cheap," he said in a groaning voice, then, bent over her as he was, began to pull his length from her slowly, "but you sold it to the right man, and that's what counts most."

With a low groan he pushed back into her, beginning to fuck the busty nineteen year old slowly.

She groaned at his words, and it sounded like she was going to bite back something at him until another moan stole her voice. Her entire body felt so hot, and she could swear she felt herself slicken at his cruel assessment of her values. She didn't *want* to sell it to anyone!

Nudging her hair out of the way, he kissed and suckled at her neck as his hips slowly pistoned into her. Gentle, the motions were pleasant, and he brought his hands beneath her, cupping her tits and squeezing them as the sound of his heavy balls slapping against her clit began to rise as his pace slowly rose.

Jarago was an excellent lover, and not because his dick was so big. Despite the slow pace he managed to strike into her at a pleasant angle, and he used his hands and mouth to such great effect upon her flesh. Titillating and provoking her nerves constantly.

She couldn't do much more than try to stay aloft, fighting against her body's desire to just collapse into a frantic state of sensations. Everything sang his praises, and her mind became hazier and hazier, replacing her anger with bursts of longing. Longing for him to go faster, to go slower, to envelope her completely. Her body was needy for him in a way she'd never experienced before, and her stomach churned with excitement.

Kissing, suckling and nibbling alternately upon her neck, the sound of his husky groans in her ear were so pleasant, another masculine sign of the man who was claiming her virginity so fully. His pace had quickened, but not to the degree part of her wished; he was still heeding her desire to be gentle, it seemed, though it didn't impede his pleasure.

As Jarago's balls tightened against him, she could hear his voice catch a little in his huffs and his body go stiff as his member went rigid, swelling within. His release was impending, and he still kept it going, drawing out the moment as long as he could.

She was familiar with the way a man's body reacts to that ultimate moment, the pleasant stiffening and bucking that rewarded her for a job well done. She had made a game out of it to see how quick she could get them to this delicious point, and she always watched their faces with awe. She tried to turn to look at his, to mentally store it away with the others, but instead he found a new place on her neck that caused her eyes to flutter shut and for her nipples to harden further against his groping hands.

His release was intense. Inside her tight quim he bucked harder than he'd ever let himself thrust in her with his attempts at gentleness, his body taking over with its automatic response. With a lewd groan that reverberated in the metal filled room, he expanded with his release, cock swelling as it lanced its rich seed into her so deeply.

Jarago bit down upon her neck a little as he emptied himself into her, his nude chest pressed against her bare back as he unleashed his entire load to the last.

Her skin prickled with the hard sensation, the feel of the erratic thrust giving her that same pleasure as men's orgasms had back in the bunker. This time, though, it seemed more intense. More rewarding as he struck against her, sending shocks through her body.

"Fuck!" she cursed, her entire nervous system attentive and teased to full attention.

As the twitching of his release subsided to the dull throbs of his post-coital cock, he squeezed her in his arms and kissed her neck. "You'll do well," he said in an approving, smooth tone of voice, that sounded very complimentary, his smooth jaw line brushing against her neck and cheek.

Her head stooped as she felt her body so near to that pivotal point and so resistant to being sent toppling over it. Even with her excitement and desire, how wet her little pussy was, and how long she had waited for this moment, her body resisted her need to cum. Even as her finger went between her thighs, rubbing slickly over that pulsing bundle of nerves, she only felt herself climb higher.

Jarago ground his cock into the sloppy cum laden mess of her cunt, his hands teasing her teats, provoking her breasts to higher pleasure as he licked along her neck and suckled her lobe. "C'mon," he coaxed, knowing what she was trying to get out of herself, "cum for me. I wanna feel you gush around my dick," he said into her ear in a lewd, harsher post-coital voice.

She felt her anger rise at his demanding tone, until she felt something much more all-encompassing crash through her. That stubborn pleasure washed through her body, leaving her shivering and thoughtless as she pressed back against him, her dainty fingers never stopping their fast, flicking action. Her breathing was so hard and her nipples felt almost impossibly tight as she felt them strain against his rough fingers.

Cramming his still turgid dick into her, he gave a satisfied 'ahhh' as he felt her warm rush of fluid announce her release upon his shaft. "That a girl," he commended, letting her ride out her release as he ground himself against her, letting his hands lavish in the supple feel of her large breasts.

When finally she slumped against him, her feet relaxing from her tiptoed position, she felt exhaustion follow in her orgasmic wake. The room stank of sex, but her mind was pleasantly, thankfully silent. She drew in long, deep breaths as she relaxed her head against the jacket, her breasts pinning his hands to the table under their heavy weight.

With a kiss to her shoulder blade, Jarago began to tug back, slipping his cock from her fluid filled cunt. "There's some food waitin' for ya if you're hungry," he said, lifting her enough to free his hands.

She suddenly remembered that she was starving, and her stomach growled loudly as she pushed herself up, clumsily reaching down for her pants. He worked a number on the young woman, but finally she was, at least, half way dressed. Her breasts were still very bare, her nipples still very hard, as she turned to look at him through lidded eyes, "Thanks."

With a confident smile he lifted his own pants back up over his hips and began to tug that monstrous sized cock back inside. "Hey, keep this up, and before long you'll have me wrapped around your little finger," he said jokingly, flashing her a charming wink as he snapped his pants shut again then reached out, giving her cheek a light stroke and pat.

Her face moved into his sweet caress before she bent down, grappling with her bra and tightening it around her chest, "Rather you didn't tell anyone about this."

With a thoughtful nod he took his hand back and plucked up his vest from the floor, "Sure, if that's how you'd rather play it," he said, getting the protective vest in position and slipping it on over his head. "I'll tell the men you're hired on as regular help then. They'll buy it after what you did to that scumbag earlier."

Tightening the clasps he added, "But, so you know, Bren'll probably figure it out eventually. Man knows me better than anyone, and he's got a thing for you, I can tell."

She nodded as she tugged her jacket on over her shirt, buttoning the bottom of it tightly against the small of her waist, "As I recall, I agreed to that portion of the deal," she said. She still sounded just as confident and sure of herself, but it was hidden beneath a mask of sleep as she went to head back out for the promised food.

True to his word again, Jarago showed no sign of what happened to the others. Returning with her to the main room he nestled up in a corner and seemed to drift off to sleep very quickly. The crew of this caravan were obviously well accustomed to sleeping through rough circumstances.

CHAPTER 5

When she awoke the next morning it was with a gentle rub of a familiar hand on the side of her stomach. Morning light hadn't quite risen fully yet and was only beginning to peek itself above the horizon, facing away from sunrise, and it was still quite dark inside the old abandoned cafe. "Come with me," Jarago said quietly.

She was not a pleasant person to wake, but she held herself in check, shutting her mouth and silencing any cruelties that were about to burst forth. Still, she was exhausted and felt the tightness in her muscles as she moved stiffly, following after her new leader. She hadn't slept well on the hard floor, and she tried to rub and stretch the kinks from her body.

Taking her with him outside, the cool morning air greeted her, though he was well prepared for it.

This time of year, with summer approaching, it didn't get that cold anyhow. Moving to one of the horses his men used, he took a rifle off one of the saddle bags, "You been trained in any weapons other than that knife of yours?" he asked, balancing the gun between his hands.

"Yea. They took my gun," she lamented. Even through the tired haze of just waking, she was surprised by his actions. She was unaccustomed to men not becoming somewhat addicted to her affections until she rebuffed them at least a half dozen times. "I'm a fair shot."

With a firm nod he shifted the rifle between his hands, "Any preference? Rifle, handgun?" he asked, looking her over all business like it seemed, much to her chagrin.

"Rifle," she moved closer, her grainy eyes trying to blink the soft light of the rising sun away. "I like something I can wrap my hands around," she teased, her eyes moving up to his face.

The business look melted as he gave a wry smile back to her, "I got just what you need then," he said, showing off the rifle, the sleek black metal of it. It was different from what she was used to, obviously constructed fairly recently, and not a holdover of the past. It was solid, sturdy, and a bit heavier than she was accustomed to.

Shifting the rifle to one hand, he trailed the other down, smoothly unzipping his pants, and saying nothing but giving her a meaningful look.

Her eyes trailed from the rifle to his hand, a smile growing on her lips as she fell to her knees in front of him. Bracing herself against his thighs, her hands squeezed him warmly before one worked to replace his and rubbing his package once more. She loved that part, the feel of it still clothed and protected from her skin. The tease of the bulge growing, and she nuzzled her nose up along it, scenting her own sex upon him.

As much as she seemed to enjoy it, he did too. His cock was already firm in his pants, though it grew further, showing despite his facade of being all business, he had his mind on her in other ways.

With his hand now free, he rested the rifle down and stroked the other palm over her blonde hair as she inhaled the aroma of his musk and her cunt still embedded upon his loins. "Glad to see you're up for the challenge of keepin' me sated," he said with a wry smile down at her. "Gal like you along, I'll be walkin' around hard twenty-four seven."

Her eyes fluttered closed as she revelled in that familiar and yet unfamiliar scent, her mouth teased along it so gingerly as she kissed. Her teeth tugged at the cloth before letting it snap back, the sensation pleasant as she quickly moved to wrap her lips around the width of his member, her tongue working against the cloth and wetting it before she finally moved her hands to remove it from its confines.

With a low, husky groan of desire, Jarago watched her upon her knees, working her mouth against his loins through his thin boxers. His hand pressed down upon her head firmly, encouragingly as the hefty girth of his cock sprang free. The shaft slapped against her face with all its heavy weight, so utterly hard with arousal as it throbbed heatedly against her flesh.

She laughed, grabbing it tightly in her palm, "So eager," she chastised. Still, as her tongue worked its way up the bottom of his cock, she seemed so natural and at home. The patterns she swirled against his skin were complicated as the wet muscle jumped along his throbbing veins, tracing along them before deviating from her path, only to wetten another heated vein. As she slowly worked her way up his length, she never stopped teasing him to absolute fullness.

Looking down at her, his handsome, smoothly dark face was lit up with desire and a bit of anxiousness; he wanted more right away. Yet he let her play, his own fingers pushing through her hair, entangling in her blonde strands as his thick cock drooled its slick precum. "What can I say," he husked in a low tone, "woke up this morning with a need that just wouldn't fuckin' die. I blame the new gal."

She flicked her tongue against his full, swollen head before her mouth finally took him in, that wet, warm hole suctioning him tight. She was still fully dressed, and her hands went to the back of his thighs, pulling him in closer as she tried to find the right tempo that made him lose control. Her brown eyes stared up at him from under her blonde bangs, and there was such lust hidden within.

She had been so repressed in the bunker, so unable to do anything but play with the men around her. And now she had someone here, fully at her command and so willing to reciprocate. She didn't imagine she'd have time for that, though. Not with the others waking soon.

Both of Jarago's hands went to her head, his large palms holding her there as he watched her move so skilfully upon his dick. With a firm grasp on her he began to piston his hips, his thick cock pushed into her mouth faster and harder. It wasn't the gentleness of last night; he knew that at this, she was a pro, and he took advantage, forcing the bulging crown to the back of her throat as he moaned into the crisp morning air. "Fuck yeah," he grunted, "god, you're good," his eyes rolled back in his head at her expert ministrations.

The way her tongue circled his head and rubbed back and forth along the shaft, how wet she was making him, it had its effect on her as well. That familiar, deep down craving that she had, until so recently, pushed aside and repressed was coming back full force as she felt the viscous liquid form from the back of her throat, her air cut short.

And still her eyes didn't move from his, focused so intently on watching his pleasure.

There was a lot of it to see, and though he tried to force his gaze down upon her, he didn't seem able to very often. Instead he bucked into her, fucking her mouth and throat, twitching as he felt his loins respond to her practised motions. When finally her skill paid off, he gasped, his smooth handsome face bunched up as he let loose a fountain of virile cum that laced across her tongue and down into her throat as he cursed her name approvingly.

She couldn't quite smile with his cock spreading her mouth so wide, but she surely looked pleased, her hands grasping him tightly and drawing him further in. It was her reward for a job well done, and she accepted every bit of thank you that he had to offer, cleaning him up adeptly with her tongue.

He still twitched and shivered with the pleasure of her mouth as she so fully laved him. "Fuck you're thorough," he exclaimed, until at last she was done and his still stiff cock slipped free of her luscious mouth.

Licking his own lips he gave a deep exhale, "Damn, hope you stick around for the long haul," he stated.

"Don't start getting thoughts on how to keep me away from saving the bunker and we'll see," she licked over her moist lips as she stood, dusting off the knees on her jeans. "Faster I get back to them, faster I can make up my own mind."

With a shake of his head he tucked himself back into his pants, leaving a sizable bulge still before he picked up the rifle. "Whatever you say," he held out the gun, "all yours for the journey. And we'll go get us some food before we head out, of course."

She took the rifle, feeling its pleasant weight as her tongue licked against her raw, numb and cum-stained lips. "Whatever you say," she echoed as she took a step away from him.

Bren was already up inside and preparing a meal. Unlike the night before, however, it didn't seem it'd be a warm one. Jarago had stayed outside, but the wide man held out a dish of some dried mix of nuts and berries to her, "Welcome aboard," he said in his deep, baritone voice, giving her a rather hopeful smile.

"Thanks," she rested the rifle aside, taking the offered food and immediately beginning to pop it in her mouth. Part of it was an effort to conceal the scent on her breath, part of it was her simple ravenous hunger. She could feel her panties, clinging damply within her slit, and she shifted uncomfortably.

The large dark haired man was caught eying her repeatedly as he ate his own, though he spoke up at last, the other two members having just left to start preparing. "Hear you'll be comin' along for a bit," he said. "At least as far as Anagio, I bet," he was bent over, elbows on his knees as he ate his own morning rations.

"I don't know where that is," she shrugged, surprised to find her food all gone, having been practically inhaled by the young, attractive woman. She leaned forward, staring at him for a long time, "I hope that won't be a problem though."

He'd been nearly done all along it seemed, and was dragging out the last few bits which he unceremoniously popped into his mouth as she got up. "It's the next stop. And no. Ain't a problem at all," he remarked, standing up, towering over her as he smiled. With a hand out he sounded a bit formal, "Name's Bren Tasler. But, y'know, you can just call me Bren of course. In fact, I'd rather ya do that."

Her smooth hand glided into his, "Alexandra," she smiled. She felt a rush of dirty excitement as their hands met, and she held his grasp a bit longer than necessary, her middle finger flicking along his palm and resting at the pulse on his wrist.

The large man didn't seem in any rush to retract his grasp either, and held her hand as long as she let him. Smiling so broadly, she could see he wasn't so bad looking. Definitely not the looker like Jarago, but his wide strong features, and the neatly trimmed hair and beard had its own appeal.

"Been a long time since we had a pretty lady along with us," he said approvingly. "And I know I ain't never seen one so good lookin'. Let alone one that could drop a Vile like you did."

"Woulda been two if you guys hadn't come along," she responded cockily as she retracted her hand, grabbing her rifle firmly. Licking over her lips, she could still taste that distinctive flavour, hidden by the morning meal, and it caused her to grin, "So you comin' or what?"

With a firm nod, the smiling giant plucked up his own stuff, "Oh yeah, boss don't like to be kept waitin'," he declared then ushered her on out.

Awaiting her outside she could see Jarago ready to go, hat in place, rifle over his shoulder, and the other two had loaded up what appeared to be two pack laden horses and another two pulling a heavy cart. "Let's go," called the handsome leader, showing no signs of the satisfaction she knew he felt from her thorough sucking.

Every step was a delicious, tortured reminder of her own need, yet she pushed it aside, letting it ferment. She craved something, so carnal and satisfying that it was hard for her to keep her eyes focused on the road ahead. She knew she had to be careful, knew it far better than she had yesterday, but still her eyes kept trailing back to Jarago, wondering at who he was, and if she could trust him. His words kept haunting her, that she'd sold it cheap, yet she had no way of knowing if it was true.

CHAPTER 6

The day's journey went by quickly. Jarago kept them all moving constantly, with few breaks, and then it seemed only for the sake of the horses and the cargo they hauled. It was a pace much in keeping with her own frenzy the day before.

Though the group kept a vigilant watch, they saw no signs of any trouble that morning.

When during one of the horses breaks, Jarago announced, "Rest a spell, gonna go scout ahead a bit."

Bren came over to her, "Now's about the only time you'll get to eat before we arrive in Anagio," he said, and produced a pouch of some more dried fruits that had been tied to his own belt.

She slumped back, the terrible night's sleep and the burning heat between her legs exhausting her.

Still, she looked fairly alert, and she gave him a gracious smile, "Oh? How long's that?" she asked.

"I like to keep some of these on hand, boss only springs for fruits and berries at the end of a trip," he explained. Then looking ahead he squinted at the horizon as if calculating, "As long as there's no trouble, only another few hours, I'd say. Close as we are, this'll probably be the last stop, knowin' the boss."

She took a handful, thoughtfully popping them past her lips, "There any place comfortable there? Is it safe? What are the people like?" she asked, suddenly realizing how abrupt she was being and blushed gently, "I'm just curious."

The giant of a man looked a bit overwhelmed by her questions, though her blushing made him smile and eased him again. He took some of the dried fruit for himself and began, only too eager to help her it seemed, "It's an okay place. Been the safest spot in the valley for years, though nowadays it's gotten a bit more tense 'round there. You can feel it off the people, harder for 'em to make a livin' off the lands outside the town with the Viles runnin' loose," he explained. "But that's never stopped 'em before, and the boss says the Viles can't keep at it forever. They eventually gotta run outta juice with how nuts they are."

"So... they're just... what? Crazy?" she asked, her face screwing up a bit, "How long have they been like that?"

Furrowing his brow he asked, "Don't you know? They've been nuts like that for way over ten years now. Ever since the old colonies fell apart," he snorted a bit, "shit, they were the reason the colony fell apart. Well," he shrugged, "them and whatever done it to 'em. Don't you know?"

"I've been in a bunker for ten years," she bit back a bit harsher than she intended. "I mean, fuck, I don't know shit about this place. And if they've been goin' at it ten years, why would they stop now?"

Bren looked a bit put off by her snapping at him, but he answered, "Yeah, but, the reason you went back into the bunker was because of the shit they caused, right? I mean... otherwise you'd have been up here with the rest of us," he explained. Then shaking his head he said, "I dunno. Boss thinks that with how savage they are, they can't be doin' too good on their own, and eventually gotta run out of new Viles attacking us and all."

"I was nine," her face screwed up a bit, "I didn't really have a lot of people clamouring to tell me about how there were psychos rampaging and killing people." Her shoulders slumped and she popped another nut in her mouth. "I kinda wish I didn't have to know about it now," she admitted, and there was fear running through her voice.

Perhaps the large man was more perceptive than he seemed, or just too used to people being upset about such things, but he reached out and placed one of his heavy hands on her shoulder. "Stay near me if trouble breaks out, I'll help watch your back," he promised.

She looked like she was about to give another smart ass response, but her true fear seemed to keep her in check and she nodded. "Yea, thanks," she popped a dried berry between her lips. "Guess you guys must be the best of the best to still be doin' this."

Bren grinned broadly at her, "Well hate ta brag but this one time–" then the call of Jarago returning broke the moment.

"C'mon, we're movin' out now," he said, looking serious and all business.

She sighed a bit, but she pushed herself up straight, grabbing her rifle firmly and looking quite serious about her own abilities of defending the caravan. Her legs ached, her muscles screamed, and her pussy pulsed, but still she carried on.

They all set off then, the rest of the team knowing the drill so perfectly. Though as they left she overheard Jarago talking to Bren. "Looks like somethin' happened at Anagio, buddy. Keep an extra special eye out the rest of the way, y'hear? Don't want any trouble before we even get to the tough part of this journey."

Bren nodded and patted his gun, "Don't you worry, boss. With the new broad aboard, I'm on the alert anyhow," he affirmed, looking deathly serious.

Her lust was a distraction, but fear was becoming a much more prominent emotion. Her gun was grasped so much tighter in her hands, and as she walked, her eyes scanned through the grass and landscape surrounding them. She knew she should feel safer traveling with the group, but nothing they had said soothed her mind.

Despite the overheard worries, the rest of the trip went uneventfully. Instead, what she saw was the curious sight of an old world city, kept alive by desperate measures.

Anagio, it seemed, was built in the ruins of a city along the river. Making use of but one part of the old place, it was nestled near the center of the valley. Tall buildings kept standing by makeshift work, metal and wood plating on the outsides, and what looked like some suspension bridges between them.

As she approached she could see the remaining tall buildings seemed to serve as guard posts around a makeshift perimeter. The real city lay inside, a mixture of old, renovated buildings of the pre-apocalypse and even some of the new, circular white buildings from the colony of her youth.

Guards manned the gates and towers, and they looked alert, guns at the ready as they approached.

She lowered her own rifle, figuring it'd be best to seem unimposing, but she never stopped looking around. Suspicion and terror had left way for curiosity, and she felt her body straighten as she tried to peer around for the other humans.

She wasn't privy to the conversation that went on with the guards, Jarago handled it before the gates–made of a mixture of wire fencing and reinforced steel–swung open for them. Beyond she got her first sight of civilization upon the surface.

Anagio sported many more residents than her bunker did, and she saw people bustling about every which way. At the sight of the caravan entering, a lot of eyes were watching. There seemed to be some anxiousness there, but the people were obviously used to hardship.

Jarago led them on through down the middle thoroughfare, and they skirted a large open market area. Looking back to her he let his pace bring him near her, "We're gonna head over to our usual spot," he explained to her quietly. "We'll set some guards on the supplies there, while I go and bargain for what we got." Looking her over in her still clean and relatively new clothes he added, "You stickin' with us still?"

"When are you guys leavin'?"

Looking around he shrugged, "A couple nights maybe," he stroked his chin and looked her over. "Judging by the looks of the place, I don't know if we'll have a hard time sellin' what we got for a good price."

She nodded thoughtfully, looking around the city, "I'm going to take a look around. Maybe someone else has heard of... Viles... stealing people's shit. Or know where I can get some supplies when I got enough to trade or whatever..." she trailed off, seeming a little uncertain. "But yea, I'll come back and check in with you soon," her eyes went back to his, those chocolate orbs intent upon him.

With a firm business-like nod he said, "See that you do." Looking her over once more he gestured to the rifle, "Hold onto that for now then. You haven't exactly worked with us enough to earn much of a cut, but you need protection," he affirmed. Gesturing over his shoulder he said, "We'll be stayin' at the inn on the north-east side. Can't miss it."

"I won't run off with your gun," she agreed, rolling her eyes in a good natured manner. Taking a step back, she paused, "There somewhere I can grab a bath?"

He nodded and pointed off towards the center of town, "Public bath house that way. Can't miss it, it's at the center of the market. Real hot spot. They don't pump hot water to many places else," he stated.

"Cost anything?" she asked.

He shook his head, already turning and going, "Public bath house is free for all," he called out.

"Great," she said softly as she turned towards the center of town. If there was something she needed, a bath was it.

CHAPTER 7

The marketplace at the heart of the little town was intense for her. She'd not seen so many people congregated in a single place since she was but a little girl. Everywhere people hustled and bustled about, occasionally bumping into her, and many breaking from their own tasks to eye the peculiar looking new woman. All about the calls of vendors rang out, though none of that hid the sight of the large bath house, just as Jarago promised. The building was pretty plain looking at its core, a large square structure, but the steps leading up to it were grand, and there were people coming in and out with towels, and the sign above clearly laid it out for what it was.

She felt her heart begin to rush, her breathing a bit constricted as she felt so many bodies press against her, but she was resolute not to let the crowds overwhelm her. The driving thought was the idea of slipping down into the hot water and relaxing, though even that wasn't the dream she'd hope it be. Immediately she found herself worrying about how and where to store her weapons as she pushed her way into the door.

As makeshift as the town looked, the bath house seemed to be something of a point of pride. It was well organized inside, clean and immediately split off into two sides, one for men, one women. Though at the juncture was a place selling clean towels and locker rentals for some local trade credits she'd never even heard of before by a woman who looked to be in her fifties.

Her nose crinkled as she stared at the woman, "I'm new here... do you guys take... I.O.U.'s? I had all my stuff stolen yesterday," she tried, knowing it was likely fruitless.

The elder woman–older than any she'd seen since she'd retreated into the bunker with the other youths in their desperate bid to survive–gave her a bit of a sceptical look. She didn't seem to buy it, or care, and she shook her head. "No handouts," she stated firmly.

"Fuck, you can have this jacket," she pushed, setting down her rifle and taking her arms out of the sleeves, "I just want to borrow a towel and put my shit somewhere safe."

With some surprise at the offer, the woman took the jacket, inspecting it as if it might turn out to be some scam, only to find it was in better condition than anything the people around here wore. Taking it and tucking it behind the counter she said, "Deal," then handed over a towel and one of the locker keys. "Bring the towel back when you're done."

"Yea, yea," she muttered as she went to seek out the lockers, bitter at having one less possession in the world.

The women's locker room was neatly arranged, and it took no effort to find the one tagged to her key. The baths themselves consisted of one large open pool and a series of shower stalls to the side.

The water, the relaxation, it soothed her to an extent she hadn't had since she left home. It was only a day and a bit, yet so much had changed. As she scrubbed the dirt and grime from her body, she left feeling fresh and rejuvenated, even without her favourite jacket. She'd be exposed to the elements now, but for the moment, it was worth it.

A long while had passed before she finally retreated from the water. Heading towards the showers she quickly washed out her panties and socks, drying them as well as she could with the towel before pulling them back on, clothing herself rather unceremoniously. Returning the towel and the key and collecting her stuff, she set out once more.

CHAPTER 8

Night was falling as she left the bath house. The marketplace was considerably slower, most of the booths seeming to have closed up. But in the dimming light of approaching evening she could make out down the street a couple places of interest. There was a shop front still lit up across from what appeared to be a bar, many people heading there at the end of their work day.

She trotted there rather quickly, the bath having rejuvenated her spunk, and her expression held the same, excited enthusiasm as it had when she first set out. Even through all her loss and the several near death experiences, not to mention bartering her virginity away - for cheap, she reminded herself - she seemed happy.

The front doors were open, and she could hear some music coming from inside. The first she'd heard since leaving home. The place was busy, and at the door a burly guard confiscated her rifle and gave her a claims chip to get it back.

Once inside herself, she could see that there was little in the way of open places to sit, but off to the opposite wall there was an open spot by the bar, nobody apparently daring to sit in it beside the tall, solidly built man there. Looking at him, Alex could almost mistake him for a much buffer, more masculine Marim. The same sort of thick flowing wavy hair that glistened under the bar light, though his skin was more tanned than her dear friends could ever get underground, however.

She was already on the lookout for people off by themselves, and she cheerily went up to the man. Her hair was mostly dry, and no longer held back in a ponytail. It flowed down over her shoulders and back, the blond colour glinting off the lights as she stood next to him, "Hey. Mind if I take a seat?"

Upon closer inspection, she could see the lighting was deceptive. His hair was a curious mix of reddish gold, that glinted blonde in the light and came about his shoulders like a thick mane. Turning towards her, she could see, once again, he bore something of a resemblance to her old friend. Handsome and appealing, he looked like Marim in the face to some degree, though his features, nose, jaw and lips, were wider.

He had a slow sort of movement about him, not as if he were dim or dull, but rather meticulous and unfazed by all around him.

With deep amber eyes he gave her a curious look over, a drink in one hand. She could see why the spot beside him was empty, in his high jack boots and tight white t-shirt that bulged from muscle, he looked and acted intimidating.

In a deep husky voice that just radiated masculinity he said, "Go on and take it."

"Awesome, thanks," she replied, her tone seeming far more girlish than usual as she slid into the seat, "Fuck, this place always this packed?"

Despite looking like he didn't care for any interruptions, the large man brought his attention back to her, slowly looking her over and nodding. "Yeah, every time I pass through," he said. Then with a brief look around he added, "Probably slower than usual, due to that raid I guess."

As he let go of his drink and took a pull on the cigar he had in his other hand, he then offered her one of his large, tanned hands. "Grent King," he introduced himself in that husky rasp of his, obviously having smoked more than a few of those cigars in what must've been at least his thirty years.

She slid her hand smoothly into his in her trademarked way, feeling out his pulse, "Alex," she smiled. "What raid?" she quickly followed up, leaning in towards him, quite interested in what he had to say.

Grent was obviously a man used to being in control, with his slow, thorough movements and the calm, assured way he sat straight and looked her over, keeping her small hand inside his over-sized mitt. Twisting in his seat slightly he lifted his hand with the cigar, looking to the bartender, "Blueberry wine for the lady," he ordered. "Town was raided by Viles just before I got here," he said to her firmly, her hand still squeezed in his.

She didn't retract it, but she smiled at his order, "Blueberry wine?" she asked excitedly before trying to shake her head free, getting back on topic, "Fuck, glad I wasn't here for that."

The man didn't hold her hand in place, letting hers slip from the rough touch of his own then returning to lift his drink. The bartender gingerly laid the wine before her, its curious blue tint showing through the dainty glass it came in. "Don't like it?" he asked, giving her another look over. "Or I guess they just don't have that where you're from, do they?" he said, as if he understood something about her without even needing to ask.

"The second," she lifted the glass, swirling it about with a curious mix of intensity. She looked at him for a moment though, her head cocking to the side, "I can't pay for it though. Just so you know."

Pushing out his jaw a bit at that declaration he shook his head and said, "Already bought it for you," and took another mouthful of his own amber drink. "And lucky you weren't here for it, yeah. Though I wish I was," he looked back to her with that intense, amber gaze of his.

She took a sip that was, at best, very unlady like. It was more of a gulp, half of it disappearing before she rest the glass down on the table with a broad smile, "They do that often? The Viles I mean."

Watching her take a gulp of the wine he simply nodded, "Yeah, they do. Not here though," he said, taking another look around the place before resting his gaze back on her. "This place was always one of the safest," he explained. "Was damn out of character for 'em too," he said, his dark voice heavy with some emotion she couldn't gauge.

"They took my bag!" she said quickly, leaning in. "I was told that was uncharacteristic too, 'cause there wasn't any food in it." She seemed so excited, as if she'd just proven her point.

Grent's brow furrowed, and she could see the man had a few marks upon his skin, old scars it seemed that traced along his jaw, and one at his forehead. They were subtle mostly, but spoke of a hard life. He contemplated her words a while before he spoke. "Hungry?" he asked, looking her over and not waiting for an answer as he spoke to the bartender, "Bring a couple baskets of dogs and fries to my usual table," and immediately he stood up, taking his drink and cigar with him.

She stood up as well, downing the rest of the wine, "You have a usual table?" she asked, trying to straighten her posture in the cramped area.

Without answering he just marched over to a corner booth directly opposite of where they were. It was, of course, occupied, as they all were when she came in, but the three young men sat there saw him coming and, with heads ducked, got up and moved out of the way before he even arrived. "I stay here whenever I pass through," he told her, sliding into his seat comfortably, as if he belonged here, or rather the place belonged to him.

She slipped in across from him, giving a passing glance to the three that made way for them, "Oh. Everyone knows you, Grent?"

With a shrug of his heavyset shoulders he puffed on his cigar and looked across at her, sizing her up in her t-shirt again. "In my line of business that's kind of a necessity." Exhaling a cloud of the gray smoke away from her he asked, "So you're sayin' one of those fuckin' freaks just came by and stole your pack?" There wasn't the disbelief on his husky voice like had been on Jarago's, instead merely curiosity.

"Yea. I came up on a building and was going to go inside when they grabbed me. There was three of them, and one took off my bag and ran off. I still don't know where they went, 'cause the other one pinned me. I fuckin' killed him, but then the other one came at me. I woulda had him too but some people came up and took him out. Still never saw the third one, but there was a woman inside the building. She's dead too."

Grent absorbed her tale passively, puffing on his cigar all the while. He didn't respond right away, but once the four baskets–filled to the brim with steaming hotdogs and fries–were placed before them, and a refill of his drink and another glass for her, he finally cut back in. "That's fucked up," he said simply and began to coat his own hotdogs in some sort of sauce from an unmarked bottle.

"Yea," she pushed herself back into the bench, thinking it all over again before reaching for a fry and popping it in her mouth. "So now I'm out here without my stuff, and I'm pretty fucked. And no one knows why they'd take my stuff so I don't even know where to look."

Quietly he pondered that, then in a series of three quick bites he'd devoured one of the four hotdogs that sat in his basket. Washing it down with some more of his drink he looked to her, "Startin' to make sense to me," he said, looking more like he was beginning to understand things in general.

"Really?" her head cocked to the side and she leaned forward, her eyes narrowing. "Wait, what do you do?"

Eating some fries as well–the man seemed to devour things at an alarming rate, but then he'd have to, to be able to maintain his muscular bulk–he then nodded, peering around them cautiously, though nobody was near them. "Mercenary, bounty hunter. Whatever you wanna call it," he said, looking her back over. "I do the tough shit no one else can. Or who has the balls to at least."

"Oh. So you... don't kill Viles or you do?" she asked, seeming a bit tense at his admission, though she noticed how quick he was eating and grabbed a hotdog before he could devour that too.

With a bit of a laugh he nodded to her, "I've killed more than I can count," he said, another hotdog disappearing with a stream of liquor going down behind it. "And I can count pretty damn high," he stated. Wiping his mouth with the back of his hand he looked her over, "And then there's you, fresh out and you've already racked up a kill or two, huh?"

Her eating paused and she stared at him, "Fresh out?" she took her wine, sipping more of it down and leaving it half full.

Nodding to her he continued eating, "You're one of the last bunker dwellers or I'm a janitor," he stated, having apparently guessed her nature by some process in his deceptively swift brain. "Those pristine clothes. Your perfect good looks. Never had a blueberry wine before," he nodded, "yeah, you're fresh out of a hole. Or from Mars."

Her nose crinkled as she looked down at the hot dog, "Oh," her lips quirked to the side, squinting a bit at him, "I guess you gotta see this stuff if you're a janitor."

That, unlike everything else, managed to crack the unflinching man. His full lips spread into a wide grin, white teeth showing at her as he gave a near silent chuckle. "You're good," he said while pointing his cigar at her a moment, "Don't even doubt your story about the Viles. You'd have taken all four by yourself in time, I bet."

She seemed pleased at his good humour, and she began to eat in earnest, "Well I only had my knife. They took my gun. The first one, that is," she pouted. "So.... why'd they take it?"

Finishing off the last of his hotdogs he looked her over, head tilted a bit, and that thick head of hair he wore barely budging with its consistency. "Viles don't steal. They kill, they rape, they pillage, but they don't steal," he said firmly. "But here they are, raidin' this town, leavin' while there's still livin' folks ta kill, and then... you," he stated, pointing his cigar at her again. "Stole from you." Mulling that over, he licked his lips, "So the only explanation is... they aren't Viles no more. Not exactly."

She cringed at the word rape, visibly pulling away before relaxing once more, though her stomach remained clenched. Yikes. Still, licking over her lips, she swallowed, "Oh. That's... not good? Good? I mean... better stealing than killing, right?"

Furrowing his brows he looked off into the distance before peering back at her. "Maybe, maybe not. Maybe it means whatever turned 'em into those fuckin' shits they are is wearin' off finally after all these years. And they are gettin' something of their humanity back," he theorized, leaning on his elbows, hands folded, the cigars smoke wafting up in front of his handsome, broad face.

"Well that'd be good, right? Except for the stealing part..." she tacked on, still sounding a bit put out by that personal loss. Her wine was gone, she had a decent dent in her food, and she was looking quite grateful at the man's kindness, even though apprehension at his words was most dominant.

It was obvious the large, seasoned man was still mulling it all over in his head. But he looked over her and the mostly eaten food–his all gone, of course–and shook his head in an unknowing look. "Maybe, but probably not," he stated. "Humans can be worse than the Viles at times. And if they're gettin' some of their ability to think and calculate back, but still got their nasty rage in 'em, then that only makes them worse. By tenfold," he added, sounding quite certain now.

"Oh," she slumped back in the bench, pushing her final hot dog towards him, "Well. You think they're gonna come back here soon? I'm here for a few days so..."

With a shake of his head he said, "I don't know that. Only puttin' the pieces together now that I spoke to you." He looked her over again then, "Where are you headed then?" he asked.

"I don't know," she shrugged. "Just tryin' to get some shit together for the people back home," she sighed. "It wasn't supposed to take long, just trade what I had, get what I needed, then come on back. Now I'm worse off than when I started."

Nodding slowly to her he said simply, "I see," then went back to pondering, puffing on his cigar now and then. "What sort of shit you trying to get together for your bunker buddies?" he asked in that same slowly calculating manner he had about everything.

She was too accepting to be sceptical of his questioning, and eagerly responded, "Food. Food and seeds and equipment to grow our own."

"You won't get that here." The statement was unequivocal, irrefutable in the way his gruff, slightly rasping voice said it. "The town's leader has ordered a halt to all trade of food and foodstuffs," he clarified. "After the raid, they can't afford to give anything away, they say. Hell, they've even confiscated what food there is from the traders, holed it away for safekeeping."

Shaking his head he gave her a slight frown, "Sorry, Alex."

"Not your fault," she sighed, though she seemed dejected. Her chin rested in her hands as she stared at him for a long few moments. "Fuck," she sighed as she pushed herself back, straightening her posture. "There's only so much I can fuckin' lose, you know."

The stoic mercenary eyed her in quiet contemplation a while. "How badly you need that stuff?" he enquired, puffing on his cigar, gears obviously turning behind those curious amber eyes of his.

"About as badly as people need to eat in order to survive," she admitted, suddenly feeling a bit guilty at the fullness of her stomach and her rejected food.

Mulling over her words, his eyes slid down at nothing in particular. Lost in thought for a bit the older man took a final puff on his cigar before stubbing it out and looking to her, "There's no other town worth a damn for trading within a week of here," he stated. "So unless your people can hold on for a couple of weeks for you to return with a big load of supplies, you have you get what you need here." The man was calculating his way through some sort of equation, she thought.

"They're already dying," Alex said, her voice lowered in some private shame. Licking over her lips, she forced herself to continue eating past the point of comfort. "If I can just get something to help them hold on while I find more... something that can get it started..."

Without another word Grent stood up, the tall broad man reaching out, pushing the baskets of food from her and taking her hand, tugging her up with him. "Don't worry about that," he said, "someone will eat it once we go."

"Oh... good," she sighed with some relief as she was tugged up, "Where are we going?" she murmured up to him, taking out her redemption chip for her gun.

He didn't go to the front door as she suspected, however, with her in tow he took her to a door at the back wall nearby, that led to a stairwell. Heading up it he kept her close at hand answering her at last as they reached the end of the first flight by pressing her between the wall and him. Despite his size and strength, it didn't seem threatening, and he left open an avenue for her to pull away. All the same, he kept a hand on her arm and looked down at her, his wide eyes a bit lidded, "Gonna take you to my room" he husked out.

Her eyes widened, more at his words than his posture, though she took a quick glance around regardless before resting back upon his face. She felt suddenly very small against him, though she realized it could be advantageous if she had to get away. Tucking her chip back in her pocket, her arms folded beneath her generous bust.

"Why?" she drawled out, holding onto the syllable like a toddler.

Sliding his hand up from her arm he released her and merely stroked his large hand over her shoulder and up to her long, blonde hair. He rested his other arm against the wall up over her, leaning his head against it as he openly admired her, "I've got more to tell you, but really because I want to be alone with you and see where that takes us." His heavy set features were relaxed, and he stroked her cheek with the backs of his fingers, "You're beautiful, perfect in fact, and I might be able to help you."

She didn't shy away from his hands and felt that familiar pulse begin to quicken between her legs. She had nearly forgotten it, but it was back with the same intensity and desire. Still, before she completely lost herself to the haze, she murmured, "I've never... before..." She didn't entirely know why she was compelled to lie, but Jarago's words rang between her ears.

Selling it cheap her ass.

CHAPTER 9

Grent's eyes widened, another rare moment of surprise and vulnerability on the large man, and Alex tried not to smile at herself. Looking over the nineteen year old, the older man paused, though didn't retreat in any way. He spoke to her quietly, his deep, rasping voice gentle, "We don't have to do anything. If I can help you or not, I'll do it regardless if you come up with me, or if we end up having sex or not," and the man, surprised as he was by her persuasive lie, sounded very genuine. His posture relaxed, became even less intimidating, and he widened her avenue to slip away.

She smiled, her face downcast for a moment before her head tilted towards where he was leading her, "Let's talk where we're not going to be stumbled across, huh?" she said softly. It was almost as though she were coddling the older man.

With a nod he led the way again, this time without taking her by the arm. Coming to the top of the stairs he unlocked a door and revealed to her a sizable room. Within it were a couple heavy bags loaded with travel goods, and by the wall a sizable automatic rifle of an old make, but obviously heavily reinforced and improved. He held open the door and gestured inside, the large bed flanked by a pair of comfortable chairs at a small table suitable for card playing.

She stood to the side of the door, just inside his room, and looked at him in a manner that seemed so demure and unbefitting the young woman. "Thanks," she smiled, the look touching her eyes, "For the wine and food and help, I mean."

Her slender fingers ran the length of her hairline, pushing some behind her ear and tracing it slightly. Her tongue ran along her lips and even though it seemed so natural, it was still so sexual.

The older man watched her motions with rapt attention, his intelligent mind mulling over something about her as he moved to shut the door. "You mind?" he asked, getting her permission before he closed the outside world off.

Stepping around her it was obvious the man was taken in, and he gestured towards the seats as he leaned in beside her, looking down upon her much shorter form. "Was worth it for the good company alone," he said lowly, reaching a hand up again lightly touching her chin with his strong grasp.

Her eyes fluttered shut for a moment at his touch, her lips curving before she took a small step away. "You don't get a lot of company?" she asked, though her voice seemed so much quieter now that they were away from the crowd.

It was obvious the large man wanted her, but since her 'admission' in the stairwell he was treading lightly. Seeing her step away from his touch he slowly walked over to the two seats, paused before reaching to the liquor cabinet there, thinking better of tempting the young woman with more alcohol, and sat himself down.

He shook his head, "And that's the way I like it, typically. Not many people interest me," he confessed.

She smiled, shimmying herself into the free chair, sitting rather comfortably while crossing her legs. "You... said you'd help me? How?" As she asked so innocuously, her thumb drew along the inside of her thigh, trying to subtly draw his attention to her body.

It didn't take much, for despite his gentleness with her since that fake confession, he didn't hide the fact he was very attracted to her. His broad chest swelled out beneath his thin white shirt, even able to see through to his areola and stiff nipples. "I've got a job tomorrow," he said to her, brows furrowed a bit. "I suspect the town leader is gonna ask me to take on the Viles somehow." Folding his hands over his lap he watched her, letting his amber gaze slip down her form, "If I take it, then that'll change the situation here. For you to take advantage."

He was something that Jarago was not – trustworthy. Honest. She was suddenly feeling very dirty for having thrown it away to the first man she'd met outside her bunker walls. "So what am I supposed to do?" she asked. Her finger found one of her blonde waves again, pushing it off her shoulder and exposing the line of her bra underneath her light t-shirt. She smelled so clean, the lingering scent of the bath still strong on her.

The older man didn't look like the brightest, with his broad features, good looks and thick muscle, but he wasn't dim. A bit surprised by her reaction he said, "Once the problem is handled, then they'll open trade again. And you'll be able to barter for what you need," he explained, licking his lips as his eyes slid down to her bust.

She sighed, as if she was hoping for something more, and she leaned back in the chair. "Oh. Yea, but still need something to trade," she murmured remorsefully, though she caught his eyes moving over her and couldn't help but smile. "Still, it's a start."

As stoic as ever, he said, "One thing at a time." She could see his thick chest rise and fall so heavily, his breathing having increased from arousal as he watched her, "When I get back from the mission, then I could help you with that part too," he stated firmly.

"Yea?" she asked, hope edging into her words. She was getting excited and her body was rewarding him with the way her legs parted slightly. She leaned forward, her elbows resting on her thighs as she stared at him, "I'm no freeloader, you know."

Uncrossing his own arms he inadvertently left exposed the sizable swelling in the groin of his own pants, his time with the youthful beauty having gotten to him quite a lot it seemed. "I'll do my best to work out something for you. And if it means I have to do you more favours than you'd like," he shrugged a bit, "we'll cross that when we come to it, Alex."

Her eyes dipped and her legs squeezed shut as if to silence her own throbbing body. She stood, shifting herself instead to the arm rest as though she were being casual, though in reality it was to feel some pressure betwixt her legs. "I guess it's not often to meet nice people out here, huh?"

Watching her, the muscular Grent's brow furrowed a bit, and it made a scar there–previously near invisible–stand out. "No you don't," he responded, and licked his lips. "But is it all that nice of me when I want to get to know you and spend more time with you?" He shrugged his broad shoulders and shifted in his spot, the usually unmovable man needing his own adjustments it seemed, "Still a bit of selfishness there."

"I don't think there's anything wrong with that," she smiled, though it looked more like a feral grin. He could see her, the way her hips just rocked so slightly as her eyes traced over his face and down his body, her lips bit in. She had been surprised by how easy it was to get him to back off, but the distance had done nothing but excite her further. He was so handsome, and strong. He was perfect for her, and shame made her blush. Why'd she lie to him?

The shifting of her hips and the way she ground against the arm rest did not go unnoticed by him, and Grent sat forward on the edge of his own seat.

Reaching out he placed a hand back on her knee and thigh, "I'll do what I can anyhow," he began, "but stay the night, here. I'll even sleep on the seats if you don't feel comfortable." He shrugged his broad shoulders, "Either way, you were robbed and you need a place to rest. Then in the morning I'll meet with the town leader, and let you know how it sounds."

Leaning forwards near her, the seasoned mercenary had lust written on his face, and looked nearly ready to burst. Only his long experience and a youth left behind could've given him such restraint, "It gets tiresome not having a special someone after a while," he added in a quiet husk.

"I'm not special," she laughed, but her legs had spread wider with the press of his hand. She was already homesick, and he reminded her of her sweet, safe friend. The one who was depending on her, and the one who was likely worried to death over her mission. The one she'd thought about becoming more with, but had always shied away from.

The one she'd return to soon, with food and goods in tow, and all thanks to this man. Grent.

His massive hand rubbed higher up her thigh, his thumb pressing in along the inner side as he watched her. "I think you are," he said simply, then got up from his place on the edge of his seat. The broad man bent over and leaned towards her, his lips moving in until he was hovered but a couple inches from her own. "We don't have to do anything. But I'd like to," he said.

She felt her heart quicken and she nodded, "Yea," she murmured. Fuck she wanted to. Even though it had only been a day, her body had a new craving that wouldn't shut up, especially not around him and his strong form. She wanted to feel him pressed against her, his weight pinning her as his mouth–

A moan escaped her as her imagination wandered, and with the heat of his body so near to her, she squirmed.

Grent took that as his cue, and the mighty man closed the gap, his head tilted as those full lips of his met hers. With one hand upon her thigh, the other coming up to rest on her bicep, he kissed her deeply, his tongue probing into her mouth and him returning her groan with a deep, chest-rumbling one of his own. His slick tongue, so much bigger than hers, felt out her mouth, and his hand squeezed and rubbed her inner thigh.

She wanted him. The way her body responded, her thighs wrapping around his legs as she tried to quiet the desire that pulsed through her. Her mouth was so hungry for his, and her lips worked hard against him. When finally she was able to breath, she pushed his chest away slightly, her breath hard.

"Lay back on the bed," she purred.

Looking surprised by her eagerness, having bought into her innocent act too deeply it seemed, he licked his lips, tasting her there as he retracted and lay back upon the mattress. As large as he was, the bed groaned and creaked beneath him, but he rested back on his palms, then his elbows, watching her intently, that wide handsome face of his framed by his strawberry-blonde hair.

She moved to the foot of the bed before crawling up between his legs. She knew she'd regret it, but there was something within her egging her on, trying to coax the fire between her thighs to new heights. She'd spent most of the day horny and wanting, and yet as her hands brushed against his package, her eyes focused on his, she felt so in control.

It was an especially intoxicating feeling, for this large handsome man who was so commanding, cool and collected before, now seemed like putty in her hands. She could see the impressive bulge of his cock pressing through his old military style pants, her fingers feeling its heat even through the thick canvas material. It swelled to her touch, giving a large push back with the automatic response.

Watching her so intently, with that same steady gaze, he reached out and stroked her blonde hair. It wasn't the condescending sort of petting Jarago gave her though. It was something more tender and appreciative, despite the man's larger size and apparent gruffness.

The smile that softened her face matched his touch. Friendly, affable and appreciative, she shifted up nearer to him and moved her fingers to the button of his pants. She didn't want to toy and tease this man, though she did enjoy his sweet touch. She just wanted to see him enjoy her body and her skill.

He was kind to her without even needing something in return, and that only made her want to give it all the more.

Grent spread his powerful thighs for her, letting her nestle between them. Usually so stoic, the broad man returned her look, though it was strange on his usually cool face. Seeing his full lips spread into a pleasant smile as he lovingly stroked her hair was a gratifying experience.

Her hands, meanwhile, undid his pants, and the dark swell of that meaty cock beneath a spandex pair of boxers lay beneath. Without even seeing it directly she could tell it would be impressively sized, even by the standards she'd so recently upped after leaving the bunker.

Even though she tried to hide that spark of excitement and impress, it was clear on her face. The way she bit in her lower lip to calm her smile, her movements were hastier. Normally she would have luxuriated in the feel of the warm cloth nestled so tightly against him, yet her hands instead delved past the barrier, lifting the large phallus out and immediately pulling back the foreskin.

Her smile was no longer to him, it was to it. Licking over her lips, she glanced at him for only a second before she lowered her body to be level with his masculinity. She visibly eye humped it, tracing every vein with her gaze before she looked back to him, the thick cock between them.

Like the man, the shaft was thick and hard. It was easily as long as the man who took her virginity the night before, but much thicker. It barely fit in her outstretched fingers, and the masculine musk that filled her senses from its unleashing was clean and palpable, intoxicating in its own right. The veins that ribbed it were bulging and full, there was barely a curve of it, but it was just right, and the crown looked dark from what she could see through the foreskin; perfectly shaped as well as deliciously huge.

Looking around the thickly throbbing shaft, so full and steely hard, their eyes met and he licked his lips. Despite his proficiency at hiding his feelings below, now he just looked at her with unadulterated fondness and desire.

She couldn't help but utter a delighted "Wow," her voice sounding full of awe and lust as her gaze went back. She no longer held herself back and pressed her full lips forward, her tongue darting out to trace up the underside of his cock. One hand kept him poised as the other struggled to further pull down his pants and boxers as she began to worship him with her mouth.

Her movements, her excitement, it was all so raw and needy, and he could tell, just by looking at her, how much she wanted him. The night before she had wanted safety and aid. Tonight he already promised her the same, and now she just wanted something more primal.

Grent couldn't help but smile at her appreciative word, though it wasn't a smug sort of expression. Instead he just seemed glad she was pleased. Lifting his rock hard ass up off the bed he helped her get his pants down over the swell of his rear, exposing the heavy ball sac that rested between his thighs.

Still stroking her blonde hair he gave a low groan at the delightful touch of her tongue upon his meaty cock. His eyes seemed to want to roll back into his head but he refused to break eye contact with her and muttered in his deep, gravelly voice, "You're the most beautiful woman I've run across in almost forty years of livin'."

"Forty?" she murmured against his cock, obviously surprised. He was one of the oldest people she'd met, yet he still looked so... good. Her teeth nipped so, so gently at his flesh as her tongue ran the length before flicking back and forth against the swollen, purple tip. She was such a little expert, and it was plain to see how much she enjoyed it.

Her gaze was focused on his as her free hand wandered along his thighs, feeling over his flesh before her thumb ran along the side of his heavy sac.

Grent King didn't seem to shy away from being honest with her, even if he did a good job of hiding his emotions before. As he stroked his large hand over her cheek and hair he gazed upon her with such a sweet expression, watching as she licked his bulging cock, pulled its foreskin back and tasted the perfectly sculpted crown, so full and well defined.

He was twice her age, and he seemed to want her to know that. "Does it bother you?" he asked in his gruff voice, his shaft twitching as her fingers grazed his sizable balls, seeming to respond to her expert attentions so well.

"No," she admitted, her brown eyes dancing with a bit of deviant delight. Her tongue swirled around the tip, then moved across it teasingly before she finally descended. Her gaze moved down as her mouth stretched to encompass him, so mindful of her ministrations as her fingers traced dotingly along his balls, simply teasing him.

It was a tough fit, all her practice before on the men in the bunker or even Jarago did not prepare her for this one man's exceptional girth. But it paid off for he groaned in some pleasant delight at feeling her warm mouth absorb the tip of his shaft.

His head tilted slowly back, and his broad chest began to swell and deflate at a faster rhythm as her fingers and mouth worked their practiced skill upon him. Those strong fingers of his knit through her hair, but it seemed more like he wanted to just be holding her somehow, and her luxurious blonde strands were the best and most convenient manner to do so.

She felt so... safe. It was a strange sensation to feel when down between a man's legs, double her age and so recently a stranger. Yet as his fingers rubbed against her head, her eyes fluttered shut and she just wanted, so badly, to make him feel good. She even ignored the throbbing between her legs, the desire to shift and let him press into her body, instead focusing entirely on him.

Alex was diligent as she worked his package, her tongue ever wet and moving, her fingers so gentle and pleasant.

The expert motions did their work, even against that seasoned, stoic man. With his heavy breathing and low groans, he clasped her head so tenderly, husking out the words, "I'm gonna cum if you keep that up." The words made it sound like he never wanted it to end, though his cock throbbed and pulsed in her hand and mouth so fully, so rapidly, she knew it wanted its release inside her then and there.

There was a brief moment of hesitation in her motions until she began once more with renewed vigour, her eyes staring at him through her blonde bangs. She needed to see his face contort with pleasure, rewarding her for a job well done. Her fingers and tongue and lips and mouth begged for his relief, even as that pulsing between her thighs demanded its own attention.

Grent's lips parted, his eyes forced shut by the pleasure she was inducing. Not even the disciplined man could resist her ministrations, his wide face contorting into one of primal pleasure. With a few lewd grunts, he looked strained as his thick dick swelled inside her mouth. It was almost painful to hold him there then like that, the added heft of his impending orgasm causing her jaw to have to widen even further.

It wasn't long before she felt it, the thick rush of seed blasting out of that large crown of his, rich and creamy. That heavy sac of his had so much of it for her in reward for her expert siphoning, and it kept coming.

She was an expert at collecting cum, but he wasn't making it easy. As her tongue worked around the tip she tried to gather it all, but some escaped from around her lips, drooling down the length of his heavy cock. Still, as soon as he finally finished, her tongue chased after it, trying to collect every last bit of his virile seed.

The seasoned mercenary looked like an army couldn't fell him, but her nimble tongue and expert lips managed it. Slumped down to the bed, breathing heavily, she had drained him. With a weary motion, he lifted his head up and looked down at her, watching her clean up the last of his thick seed. He stroked her hair so tenderly. Such a strange turn, for until she professed her virginity in the stairwell, he seemed primed to aggressively seduce her, yet her perceived innocence had brought something out in him.

"That was amazing," he said in his gravelly voice, weariness lacing his words. "I've never had one so good as that."

Her lips were numb, and she crawled up alongside him. She wasn't a cuddler, not by a long stretch, but her hand rested on his chest, her head settling against his bicep. It was different with him. "That's because most people are lazy," she murred quietly. She was right next to his face, and he could feel the warmth of her voice across his ear.

She had no clue what his day had been like prior to her running into him, but having drained his balls of his cum, leaving his cock slowly softening against his thighs, she could hear and feel the weariness on the man.

All the same, he put his strong arm around her, welcoming her against him only too comfortably, giving her a place to rest against his hard body. Leaning in he kissed her lips fully and without any reservation, not troubled by the taste of his own seed on her lips and breath as others might be.

Bringing his free hand over to stroke along her hip he said in his husky, low voice, "I wanna return the favour," and gently, but firmly he began to press her back towards the bed. Not even the exhaustion the powerful man felt deterred him from his generosity.

She looked about to argue, but that throbbing need between her own legs finally silenced her objections and her fingers were already working at the buttons on her jeans, shimmying out of them with some trouble, trying to get the tight material over the round swell of her ass. She was practiced, however, and they finally gave way, resting mid-thigh.

The way she looked at him was so desirous, and so grateful at the same time.

Having shifted her onto her back, Grent brought his strong hands to her thighs, curling his fingers into her panties and jeans then pulling them down off her legs with an ease of strength only he could manage. Laying them aside he then stroked his rough touch over her two legs, and she could see the deep appreciation on his face for her smooth, unblemished flesh as he felt them out.

It was like every part of her was some new, magnificent discovery for the man, and as he parted her two legs he kissed along her soft inner thighs, he—like her—didn't tease over long. She was so slick, so ridiculously wet from a day of denied desire, that the scent of her womanhood was like a drug to him. It invigorated him even as the man's post-coital weariness fought to make his eyelids droop.

Pressing her thighs back, Grent brought his mouth to her at last, his broad tongue lapping over her slit and tasting her femininity as he coaxed her needy clit to pleasure.

That sudden, heated spark caused her to shift, her breath catching in her throat. Her t-shirt and bra felt suddenly so constricting, and her fingers lifted the light cotton top over her head, tossing it to the side and tussling her long, wavy hair in the process. He could see the smooth line of her stomach, the soft, unexposed flesh and the two mounds hidden beneath the white, lace bra.

Her breathing was faster, and as she struggled to undo and discard her bra, her feet moved to his back, drawing him in. The light blonde hair that his nose nuzzled to smelled like denied sex, and even the insides of her thighs seemed lightly glossed with her femininity.

With his own cock still out and exposed, he was bent between her legs, showing her an impressive devotion and skill of his own. In his lifespan that was twice her own, he'd obviously had practice at this, so as he gripped her thighs, and her heels dug into him, he tongued her clit quite expertly. Such a large, damp muscle it was, it had no trouble hitting the tender spot of her slit anyhow.

He was so devoted to his task of eating her cunt out, his eyes were shut almost the entire time, but as her heavy breasts were freed not even his commitment could keep him from gazing up at them longingly.

It was made worse as her own hands went to them, her body arching and her own eyes fluttering shut as she teased those twin nipples, tugging on them before letting them snap back to her chest, only to repeat the process. It was such a delightful view, and one so few had the pleasure of seeing.

She was built so high, neglected for what felt like an eternity, and his skill was quickly bringing her to that breaking point. She was already so wet, her labia parting against his strong tongue and that exposed bud throbbed against him. Her heated sex burned against his face, blood rushing from her mind and filling that one, central part of her before she gasped, her back arching just as he hit her that one, final time.

As if in reward for the delightful sight of her toying with her own tits, he didn't cease, however. His tongue and mouth rode her quim through that finale, lashing at her mercilessly. Grent seemed intent on milking from her every ounce of pleasure she'd allow, his powerful tongue and jaw working her cunt as his hands stroked her thighs, and his eyes gazed up, soaking in the sight of her own pleasured face and heavy, aroused tits as he was covered in her honey.

It wasn't long before her bucking became a serious impediment to teasing her over sensitive clit, and her gasped moans and cries echoed off the room as her foot moved to his shoulder, kicking him away. Her face was red and her bangs were matted to her forehead as she gulped for air. Her lips and mouth felt so dry and she constantly tried to wet it, staring at him in awe.

"Holy fuck," she moaned, sitting herself up after what seemed like a long while.

His face coated in her juices, he licked around his lips and wiped his cheeks with the back of his hand, before then licking that clean too. With a broad, weary smile, he stood up, his cock only partially turgid now, but still looking so perfectly grand.

Tugging his pants down and his shirt off, she could see the man fully nude. His bulk wasn't the perfectly chiselled look of a bodybuilder, but instead the look of a man whose muscle came from hard work alone. His chest smooth but thick with muscle, he was peppered with scars, big and small, and a spattering of hair that matched his head.

Pulling back the blankets on the sizable bed, he scooped up her naked, weary form then climbed in, laying her out beneath the sheets before sliding in beside her, arm around her. He was intent on keeping her closely pressed to him.

She didn't fight him. Suddenly she found she didn't give a fuck about the outside world, or of men who only wanted her to keep them happy. A small swell of rage rose in her chest but it was quickly snuffed out as she felt the weight of his heavy arm around her, his hard body heating her and holding her tight.

It was the same feeling of affection and safety, and as she drifted off, she had a hope that things would work out okay for the bunker.

CHAPTER 10

The next day began when the mighty man beside and around her tried to quietly disentangle himself from her without waking her. It didn't work however, and so she saw his broad face, graced with another slight smile as light poured in through the window upon them. "Breakfast'll be brought up soon," he said in his gravelly voice, leaning over and kissing her lips again, none of last night's tenderness having worn off on the man as he squeezed her in his thick arm.

Again her bitchiness was kept at bay, all the more so with the promise of food. Still, her forearm draped across her eyes as she moaned, her lips kissing him back of their own accord. "Fuck," she murmured, feeling that strange dried slickness between her thighs and shifting her legs. "Goin' to need another bath."

The morning sun lit up the man, his tanned face and chest. It illuminated the scars as well as his most handsome features in a soft glow, but it all came together to only make him look more rugged and appealing. Stroking a hand over her side and hip, another came up to do the same to her cheek and hair. "After breakfast I gotta go meet the town leader, like I told you last night. If you can't wait," he shrugged lightly, "you can go then. But I'll probably take some time to do it myself today too."

As the large man pet and held her so tenderly, she could feel the heat and thickness of his cock beneath the blankets pressing against her leg as it draped over one of his thighs. The morning had gifted his impressive girth with a steely rigidity.

"Had to give up my jacket last time," she sighed groggily, rolling onto her back, though she shifted back against him almost immediately. "Fuck. I really liked that jacket too," she groaned remorsefully, her eyes staring at the ceiling as she noticed that telltale throb against her thigh.

Even with her messy hair and her pillow creased face, she was a beauty. It was almost endearing to see her in such a fresh state, to see the little unaccounted for flaws.

The large man watched her with a certain placidity, though behind his amber eyes burned desire that she could easily read, and something more. Stroking and touching her tenderly with his hands he leaned in and kissed her forehead, "I'll take care of that," he said huskily. "Wouldn't be right to have a lady walking around without a bath or jacket."

She laughed, the sound genuine if a bit husked with sleep, "I don't think I've been called a lady before." As soon as the words were out of her mouth she grew hot against his body, biting her lip roughly.

Leaning forward he gave her the sweetest, most loving kiss she could've imagined. The large man pressing their mouths together and luxuriating in the feel of their lips united. It wasn't anything particularly passionate or artful, it was just tender and caring.

Despite his hardness and desire, the timidity born from her 'confession' of virginity seemed in him still, and he made no moves to press anything on her sexually, no matter how hard his body ached for her as she could plainly feel. Instead he continued stroking her side, along her large breast and down to her hip. "I think you'd make a perfect lady for the right type of man," he said, his usually gravelly voice all the more so from having just awoken.

Her hand ran across his shoulder and she tugged him close, pressing her body against him. "How long we have?" she murmured into the bed of chest hair, snuggling into him so warmly. As her hand moved down over his side, running to his back, her nails tickling him.

"Any moment now," he husked, his own hands returning her touch, feeling out over her perfect flesh, the fair skin that contrasted to his own deep tan and hard hands. From her thighs up over her hips and ass, across her tits, again and again he felt her, kissed her lips, cheek and neck, "She'll knock then leave the food outside the door as usual."

She nodded as she returned his affections, tracing along his flesh first with her fingers, then with her mouth, then with her tongue. The way her body shimmied and pressed against him, how her thighs parted and then re-converged before she shifted and suddenly had her leg draped over his hip, she seemed so desirous of the man, and she was.

He was kind and respectful and so, so hot. Perhaps it was just that he looked so familiar, yet so different and foreign, but the way his body was responding to her was only too encouraging.

The man responded to her movements so quickly, his broad chest heaving as he returned her touches, grinding his thick cock against her stomach and mons, with a smear of his precum against her. As his hand gripped one of her round ass cheeks he husked into her ear, "You don't need to do this. I want it bad, but you don't owe me your first time," and gave her a serious look.

A knock came at the door then, the food delivered outside, and the sound of the server shuffling away coming thereafter.

She was starting to regret telling him that, but she shook her head, her mouth tracing along his jaw. She wasn't a liar by nature, and there was a ball of guilt in her gut.

"Fuck it," she purred, her tongue flicking against his earlobe. "Better you than some creep." There was a soft bit of remorse edging into her words but she silenced it with a long, suckling affection of his neck. She was so soft against him, every part of her so well-crafted to be in contrast to him, and he could feel just how wet she'd gotten, even in the few moments since waking.

It was hard for her to read him, hard for anyone, but she could see then the look of satisfaction and gratefulness on his face at her words. He wanted her bad, and no amount of chivalry or kindness changed the fact that he yearned for her. Kissing her neck, he squeezed his two thick arms about her as he slid her smoothly into position beneath him, his own large body rising up over hers, between those delicious thighs she had that so intrigued him last night. "I'll take it slow and easy," he promised as she felt the surprising heft of his cock rest against her slit.

She nodded, though really she didn't need his reassurance. She knew he'd be respectful, and that made it all the harder to keep misleading him. Still, it seemed to change something pivotal in him, and she liked what had become of it. Her mouth found his, silencing him as he could feel her body warm and wetten for him. Her chest pressed hard against him and her breathing quickened as she drew his body weight onto her.

Grent's large form pressed into hers, and with it the bulbous, wide tip of his cock began to part her folds. It was harder to accommodate than even her first but a couple days before, the man's large size making all the difference. True to his words, however, he eased that thick shaft into her, his tongue probing her mouth as he gave a rumbling, low groan of pleasure as her tight, slick canal greeted his dick.

She was so wet, and it helped ease his entry. The warm remains of the night before mixed with the heated dreams and the passionate wakeup call had stoked her fires once more, and her legs parted to make way for his thick shaft.

It was, somehow, everything she had actually hoped her first would be. In a bed, in private, with a warm, strong body pinning her down and heating her up. Her mouth worked more eagerly against his, begging him silently with each curve and caress.

Though their mouths were sealed upon one another, it didn't keep the large man pressing down upon her from letting out his own low satisfied groans as he claimed her virginity; again. Grent was so emotive, the stoic man taking such pleasure in her as his girth sank in deeper, until the wide crown was pressed fully against her utmost depths. So large was he, he couldn't fit the entirety of his shaft inside her, but he lingered there and seemed to find it immensely pleasurable.

He allowed her time to adjust, and cupped one of her breasts by the side, brushing his thumb over her nipple between them as he kissed and fondled her.

She moaned against his tongue as her hand pressed against his back, rolling down towards his ass before she grazed her nails across it. She felt such a pleasant warmth all around her, fuelling her desires as she felt that stiff shaft lodged so deep within her. It was the feeling she'd waited for so long, and the entire scene was just as she'd hoped. She'd pushed it out of her mind, the quick time before. As exciting as it had been, the dirtiness was incomparable to the tenderness of this moment.

Grent lingered in her unmoving, kissing and touching her. Though the large man took his time, however, his organ felt differently. The thick shaft lodged in her depths throbbed and swelled wildly, pushing her already stretched canal out wider.

When finally he began to tug back his hips, his hard ass pushing against those nails, he gave a lewd grunt. She was heaven around him, and he seemed blissfully happy with being inside her, being her 'first'.

Her hand followed the rise and fall of his ass, her other fingers pressing into his neck and rolling down over his shoulders as she started to gasp and moan. She had been mostly silent against his mouth, but the second he released it, she was noisy and needy with tiny grunts and whispers of desire and pain and ecstasy combining into something so primal. Despite his girth and how wide he spread her slick pussy, her hand egged him on, pressing down on his ass and encouraging him.

The gentle Grent resisted her urgings however, his thick cock continuing to make its way achingly slow into her pussy again and again. His heavy balls gave light slaps against her damp ass crack.

Looking down at her through lust-laden eyes, he asked her in his deliciously masculine husk, "Are you sure you can handle it?" His gorgeous chest, peppered with hair and the marks of a lifetime spent in harshness displayed before her as that wide shaft plunged in and out of her.

She didn't realize she had been biting her lower lip, but as she let it pop out, another loud groan followed, and she nodded eagerly.

"I want it," she said, sounding so breathless and sincere. She wanted it worse than anything else she'd craved in all her life, and her brown eyes were focused on his.

The shift was done so smoothly, so expertly, it was a beautiful transition. Grent's powerful hips began to plunge his meaty cock down into her faster, a little harder. It was obvious the strong man was in perfect control of his every muscle, and he pressed himself into her just right, the slap of his balls striking her wetly now filling the room as the blankets slipped away from them both.

Leaning down he kissed her again and seemed caught up in a deep passion for the young woman. He was grunting and groaning so harshly from the pleasure her perfect form was giving him.

Her breathing was so much harder as she felt his stiff body press against hers more readily, and her thoughts began to blur and drift away. All that was left was the passion and bliss of the moment, the intensity of his body weight atop of hers, and the exhilaration of the act itself. As her legs lifted to wrap around him she felt him move into her more deeply and her breath caught before a loud moan of pleasure pushed it past her lips.

"Fuck," she gasped, her vision blurring a bit, "Fuck," her hips tilted a bit more and she felt it again, that shock of intense pleasure.

Grent smiled, deeply satisfied to see her so overwrought with pleasure atop his manhood. Squeezing her in one arm, her breast in the other hand, he never let up. His shaft continued to piston into her at that exquisite angle as he watched her writhe beneath him. Leaning his head down, careful not to disturb his smooth rhythm, he kissed her lips, her jaw, her neck, adding little bites to her sensation overload.

The curses all started to trail one another as she clenched the sheets beneath her, eyes shut tightly before finally she gasped, a scream of ecstasy following it and reverberating off the walls. Her head bounced back against the pillow and her body arched just so, bringing her breasts to his chest and pressing against him so tightly. That soft flesh, those hard nipples were held so firmly against him as she rode out the intense wave of bliss.

The flood of warm honey that coated his girth was exquisite, the spasming grasp of her canal all the more. Clenching his own jaw he arched his head back and pressed against her, refusing to let up as the whole of his own broad frame quivered and shook from his own enjoyment of her pleasure.

With a grunt and a gasp he husked out, "I want to make you feel that again and again."

His words were so sweet to her, but she barely was able to make out what they meant. All she knew was this man was someone good, and she wanted to feel him fill her. As she relaxed back into the bed, her body still felt the sparks of pleasure. She stared up at him, "You can cum in me," she whispered, knowing the device within her kept her body regulated, and pregnancy at bay.

Through it, Grent's motions had never ceased. He kept up that pleasurable thrusting, never losing the tempo or precise strike. Her words took him by surprise, and she could see it in those almond-shaped eyes of his as they widened. "Y'sure?" he asked in a gravelly voice, his dick responding to her with such wild swelling throbs, the man reaching his hand from her back to her hand, taking hold of it firmly.

"I'm safe," she sighed out, her mouth finding his once more. Her motions were a lot slower and less skilful, but lacked none of the passion or desire that recently coursed through her. Her muscles clenched against his swell, and her hand rested against his lower back.

The combination of her words, the sweet invitation, and the delicious feel of her quim tightening around him, was all he needed. Holding her hand tightly, he pressed himself upon her and gave her a few more thrusts before he erupted with pleasure. The large man gave such a brutish groan of satisfaction it broke the seal of their lips, his face looking more intensely pleased than when her skilful tongue siphoned his seed from him the night before.

With each spasm of his cock his hips bucked, and he unloaded himself into honey slick canal with long pulsing throbs. And through it all on his husky voice he muttered her name clear and adoringly.

His orgasm awakened her once more and her kissing across his chest and neck was more frenzied and passionate, letting out soft sighs and moans of pleasure as she felt him hit so deeply within her sensitive cunny. When finally he came to rest, she was slick with their combined sweat, and her face was flushed with excitement.

Releasing her hand and breast as his loins stilled within hers at long last, he scooped her sweaty, satisfied form up into his two arms, nearly crushing her against his hard body as he embraced her. It was tenderness, desire and something deeper, an emotion so strong in the large man he just had to hold her tight and cup the back of her head as he lifted her off the bed with his adoration.

Long locks of strawberry blonde hair tickled along her neck and face as he kissed her, not wanting to let her go for a long time.

For some reason, she let him. Though usually she wanted very little to do with someone after she'd gotten what she wanted, she found she hadn't yet. Not with him. Not from the orgasm, not from the sex. It was a softening of sorts, a desire for the close comfort of actual intimacy.

Still, there was only so long the feisty girl could remain lodged next to the hulking man and as her stomach rumbled, she pushed him away with a disarming smile.

Pleasantly he returned her look with his own, his broad face lit up with a warm, loving smile. Twice her age and a life spent in the harsh wastes of the old world hadn't erased his appeal; it had only added a certain ruggedness to his natural good looks, and the emotion written all over his face doubled it up again. "Lay right there," he said in his deep voice, "I'll bring it to you," and he pulled away from her reluctantly, his still large cock slipping from her damp folds as he moved to get up.

The wetness was strange, and it felt cool and warm all at once as she tugged up the blankets over her naked body. Licking over her lips, she watched his back as it moved, and her body twitched in response.

"Fuck I'm hungry," she said light heartedly, as if to spoil the tender mood.

Unabashedly he went to the door after she covered herself, and reached out, lifting up the tray off the floor and shutting the door. Tall and muscular, he walked back, carefully laying out the large platter before her, "I never told 'em to send up two meals, wasn't plannin' on having company," he said, "but don't worry, I can get more later, so eat your fill." The generosity of that statement seemed somewhat lessened when he uncovered it to show enough food to feed four people, including a mound of fried bacon that was startling.

"Uh... yea, you can... share with me," she smiled, even as she began to eagerly eat, not having been lying about her hunger. "You taking off soon?"

Climbing back upon the bed, over top of the blankets, he began to pluck some of the strips of meat and inhale them faster than he had the hotdogs the night before. "Yeah," he nodded, using his free hand to lightly stroke her hair, "if you got things to do, I'll meet up with you after to tell you what's up."

"Yea, I gotta check in with some folks... probably get a bath if... I could... borrow some credits or whatever it is they use here," she asked sheepishly. "I'll pay you back, I'm just... I can't really walk around stinking of slut, you know," she teased. "Think there's anything else I should do?"

Nodding to her words he put his free arm around her, devoured another piece of bacon then hugged her close and kissed her forehead. "I'll tell 'em to give you a key to the room too. I'll keep it on my tab for as long as you need a place to stay here," he said.

"You're somethin' else, aren'tcha," she grinned, trying to keep up with his eating pace and failing dismally. "Thanks. Really. Fuck, it's good here... close to home. If I can get what I need..."

As generous as the man had been, there definitely seemed a change in him now and the way he offered–or simply assumed–help to her. "What good's credits and influence if you can't use it to help the one you care for?" he said, kissing her lips then slipping from the bed to stand abruptly and grab for his clothes.

Her face brightened at his encouragement, finishing off what she could of the platter before trying to find her own bra, dressing rather sheepishly. "So I'll find you in the bar or what?"

Though he often moved so slow, he was dressed in almost no time. When he wanted to move, it was with a swiftness of purpose that belied his great size. Buckling his pants he nodded to her, "Down there or up here, sure," he said.

Pulling his shirt on over his head he grabbed a jacket from a hook then slipped his hand around to the back of her head, leaning down and kissing her forehead again. "Then we'll see about getting you a new jacket too," he promised, slipping a pouch full of what must've been the town's trade credits. Sliding his palm to her cheek he looked her in the eyes. "Afraid to say it, but I think I love you," and the words weren't flippant or joking, purely sincere, and followed by a passionate kiss before the man turned to leave.

The wastes were a hard place, and people lived fast or not at all. She'd learned that even in the last day, and understood why he was in such a hurry to declare something that the folks in the bunker would hem and haw over for months.

Still, she was too dumbfounded to stop him, and by the time words finally formed on her lips, he'd already gone down the stairs. Stepping backwards to the bed she looked down at the pouch in her hands curiously.

"Huh," she murmured to herself as she set it aside, finishing dressing before tucking it into her pocket, locking the door as she left back into the new day.

The town was already going by the time she got outside, the tavern manager had given her a key to the room, just as Grent had said and she had enough credit to see about a bath and then some.

When she was clean once more there was an extra spring to her step, and she seemed almost jubilant. For some reason, she really trusted Grent to follow through and be able to solve all her problems, and yet that wasn't enough for the plucky young woman. She was still quite intent on ensuring that the lives of the friends she left behind would not be hindered, and she quickly moved her way through the town, looking for someone selling food.

The food vendors on the street–true to Grent's warning–were not able to sell her large amounts. They were all on strict orders to only give out food with vouchers from the local government, which basically comprised of the town's leader and family. The only way around that was to buy food through the hotels or inns, and even then they would not supply more than a meals worth cooked, or enough for a bit of travel.

When enquiring about what sorts of things the traders themselves liked in return, she was given a large number of options. Trades in the town tended to differentiate, but anything with value, technology, components, animals, clothes, tended to be in demand. Weapons were a high priority item, as the guards tended to monopolize most of the goods in that area. She noted this all in her implanted computer device for later.

As she was finishing up talking with one final vendor, she caught sight of a familiar face. Jarago came out of the crowds, hands in his trench coat as he looked her up and down. "So you haven't run off," he said, coming up to her. "Was wonderin' where the hell you went last night," he said.

"Oh hey," she smiled brightly, not a trace of shame on her face. "Just tryin' to make some connections, you know. See what the fuck I can do to make sure everyone's goin' to live. How're you guys holdin' up? Apparently the Viles attacked yesterday, that's why everyone's all antsy."

Casually Jarago walked up by her, then took hold of her arm, guiding her away. "Well on that front I got some good news for you," he said, speaking a little quieter as he led her down a side street. Looking her over he said, "Was gonna let you in on the good news last night, but you never showed up. Where the fuck did you end up sleepin', anyhow?" He sounded a little annoyed, as if she'd rebuked some offered kindness.

"In the inn," she said, as if that was a foregone conclusion, "What's the news?" She was looking so clean and fresh after her bath, and that smile she wore was just for him. If anything, she was a skilled temptress.

"The inn?" he said, "I had a fuckin' room in OUR inn for you, and you weren't there." He took her off into a side alley where it was dark and barely any light trailed in. Coming to a stop he kept his hand on her arm and looked her over, "Had plans for last night, ya know. You still owe me, accordin' to our agreement." Her pleasing smile wasn't lost on him, for as he looked her over he licked his own lips.

"Sorry," she murmured, sincerely as her eyes dropped down. "I didn't know. I figured you guys were doin' your own shit or whatever. It's not like I've done this before, you know," she added on, sounding a little bitter at that.

As crass and uncaring as he could be, the slender man was looking more attractive than ever. The time in town had given him time to clean up too, and he was wearing a nice shirt beneath his jacket that was undone to about halfway down his dark chest, his hair and face well cared for. All of that only proved to distract briefly though as his hand went to his fly, undoing the zipper, "Got an important meeting soon, need your help unwinding real quick," he said.

"Alright," she agreed, easily, as her hand went immediately to his package. Her rifle was held in her other hand, careful of the priceless object even as she went about teasing the other man to fullness. Even with the tension between them, it only seemed to egg her on and become a bit more malicious and spiteful as she stared up at him, "Missed me, hmm?"

Jarago took a look up and down the alleyway casually before looking back down at her as if confused by her question. "Yeah sure," he said. His cock was soft when she first got a hold of it, but it started to stiffen to her touch immediately, the dark shaft lengthening and growing in her grasp. "Was gonna bust out some whiskey and have a good time with you last night, you missed out," he said.

She smiled a bit darkly as she dropped to her knees, her motions so skilled even as she hurried to work him to excitement quickly. She really would rather he not be pissed off at her, after all, and if there was one thing she was good at, it was making guys forget they were mad at her. "Fuck, I wish I had known," she purred and he could feel her warm breath against his package as she worked his cock towards her mouth.

She pushed Grent and his kindness and love from her mind and focused on this, on him. She trusted the other man, but lives were at stake, and if Jarago might have a connection for her, it was worth a simple blowjob in a back alley.

Her stroking had taken his cock from soft to full in but a few seconds. He was pulsing with heat as his hardness throbbed in her hand and he reached out, patting her head in that familiarly condescending way. "Should've come back like I said," he reiterated. "Now make it good, we don't have a lot of time," he prodded.

"I'm always good," she promised as her mouth suctioned around his cock. She was used to these clandestine meetings, the public nature of such things, and usually she was so good at being discrete. This time, however, she was working with such furor and intensity that her surroundings didn't matter at all. She was intent on getting him off as quickly as possible, and everything about her motions pleaded with him to hurry.

The sleazy scene in the dark alley went by in such a tawdry manner. Jarago took hold of Alex's hair and head in both of his hands, helping move her mouth upon his cock faster. Despite the nature of their little tryst, he didn't do a good job of being quiet. The man groaned in pleasure even as feet tread on by unbeknownst to them both.

She could feel the hot flesh of his cock swelling in her mouth as he gripped her hair, "Fuck," he cursed, "suck it out."

She rolled her eyes a bit, even as she enjoyed his vulgarity, and clamped her mouth around him tightly as her hand grabbed him, coaxing her to the back of her throat. Eyes watering, saliva pooling, she felt him swell within her and she prepared for the onslaught.

The man was rough with her as he bucked his hips, giving a series of noisy 'ah's' as he pumped his load into her throat. He had to let go of her head towards the end, to rest a hand against the grim back alley wall to hold himself up, though he didn't need to be egging her on with it in the first place, for her expert lips were suctioning his seed out of him so gloriously without his interference.

"Oh fuck yeah," he cursed as she drained the last of his load away. "Good goddamn job," he swore, licking his lips.

When finally he finished and she swallowed his seed, she was red faced and gasping for breath. Pushing herself up from the alleyway, she looked at him with a bit of hardness to her eyes, though it was tough to see as her forced smile seemed so genuine, "You said you had good news for me."

Tucking himself back into his pants he nodded to her, "Yeah, c'mon." He started walking back out of the alleyway, talking as he was going. "You need to negotiate trade for your people, right?" He said, sounding like he was finally taking her situation seriously. Or trying to sound like he was.

"Yea, for food and stuff," she agreed, curious to see if he knew about the situation in town or if he'd be honest with her about it. She followed – or rather, was dragged – along, looking up at him as he spoke.

"Well," he said, giving her a cocky smirk, "just so happens you sucked the right dick." The man knew no shame and she tried not to roll her eyes. "I can get you a chance to speak with the head of the town. The best and maybe only man who might be able to get you what you need. How's that for good news?"

"How'd you manage that?" she asked, awe and scepticism mixing in her voice. She'd left her long hair down once more, and it flowed behind her as they moved, and she was just the faintest bit annoyed that he hadn't noticed her lack of a jacket.

With a casual shrug of his shoulder he said, "I'm meetin' with him to discuss a trade of our guns to his guards. As you pointed out, the town was raided, and they need more equipment. Bad. So… I'll take you along. Introduce you. And well, the rest is up to you, sugar." He gave her a smarmy grin, "The man likes pretty women. And you know how to get what you need."

She resisted the urge to roll her eyes, instead staring straight ahead. She seemed rather deep in thought for the rest of the way, not talking much, but her pace seemed a bit quickened and more determined and there was a flush of anger beneath her skin.

This was just what she was afraid of back in the bunker, having everyone there think she's nothing more than a slutty hole to fill. It was the reason she'd held on to her virginity so long in the first place. Worse than her anger at Jarago, though, was the shame she felt at the new heat that was growing in her loins at the thought.

The building they were going to was without a doubt the largest in the town. One of the new, circular structures that were from the re-colonization attempts a decade ago, it still looked pristine and new, unlike the older, refurbished structures about the place. They had to pass several guards, and Jarago had to explain his purpose and provide a letter to one woman before they were finally let into a waiting room.

Leaning over to her in his seat, he said, "Keep quiet until I introduce you, sugar. I know how to deal with this guy." She didn't have much time to respond for the secretary opened the doors into a large circular office and waited for them to head in.

She was going to tell him not to speak for her and not to say anything without her go ahead, but in the whirl of doors and people, she never got a chance. *Please don't be an asshole*, she willed him, staring at his head, *Don't offer me up like I'm some whore.* She knew it was useless, even if she did say it aloud, and the way her stomach churned was making her regret ever running into him. She didn't trust him, not like Grent. Even if he was helping her.

The room inside made the bunker she grew up in look Spartan by comparison. It was in many ways similar, but not only was this the only place in the world above she'd yet seen that looked clean, it was also opulent. Old world items were assembled and fixed up, even a few pieces of technology that seemed to work, like a computer.

Though behind the desk was a man–a little shorter than Jarago–but with milk-chocolaty smooth skin and long, sleek black hair that was streaked in a few places with white. The man had to be a good ten years older than Grent at least, though he looked well, aside from the round, black glasses he wore.

Standing up he gestured them to the seats in front of his desk, "Come in," he began, his voice having some strange accent to it she'd never heard. "Take a seat and be comfortable," when his dark brown eyes turned to her she could detect something there in his gaze as he looked over her. "A new assistant?" he asked.

Jarago butt in immediately, "Yeah, she's just joined my team in fact," he said. "Alex, this is–"

And the older man stepped around his desk, dressed in a formal shirt with tie, vest, black pants and shoes like out of some old photo. "Dr. Kenir Feysar. A pleasure, madam." He took her hand without much delay, smoothly kissing the back of it like some gentleman out of a movie.

Even though mentally she was annoyed, it was nearly impossible to tell. In fact, she looked practically coquettish as she tilted her head down and to the side, as if paying respects to someone far better than her. Her body language changed and became more submissive and accommodating, and she made even the simple t-shirt and jeans look amazing with the way she arched her spine to bring out the curves of her breasts and ass.

If he was going to be an asshole, she was at least going to get what she wanted on her own terms. She wasn't going to leave anything to fate.

The aged doctor, as he called himself, stroked a thumb over her hand and lingered his dark brown eyes upon her a while before finally Jarago interrupted, "About the weapons then, chief. We got a full load, but they're already promised to the next town we're set to visit."

She noticed then a curious thing. The leggy woman who served as his secretary looked quite similar to him, and was very likely a relative of his.

"Ah," the doctor said, slipping back and sitting on the edge of his desk, "now that would be a shame." His eyes turned back to her though, and the elder man smiled right at her even as he spoke to Jarago, "I think we can offer a price that will accommodate for your lost deal and the fallouts from it."

She didn't remain still, her eyes and face turning and looking around the room, as if not entirely listening to the boring talk of business, though she very much was. She gave a smile to the secretary, then remembered what some of the traders had said about the town being run by a family. It made sense.

The two men talked over terms and prices a while, and it got tedious, though one thing she couldn't ignore was the way the elder gentleman's eyes remained on her. Even to the detriment of his negotiating position.

When finally he shook hands with Jarago with an agreement, the pale-blonde caravaneer said, "Well, I've gotta be headin' on to see to that then. If you got anythin' else you need," he pointed to Alex, "just let the assistant know, and she'll inform me." He smiled and left, the secretary closing the door behind her and the retreating Jarago.

She hated being left alone, but walked up to his desk rather brazenly, "Hey, so. I'm not here about guns or whatever," she smiled a bit, leaning down and placing her hand on the desk casually, facing him. "I have a bunker of friends that are dying, and I need to get them food. Someone stole all my trade goods, and I'm up shit creek without a paddle. Since you're the big shot around here, I hoped you'd have some ideas."

The way she drew her pink lips into her mouth, that angle that let her hair spill down over her face was all so practiced and controlled as she tilted it demurely.

The dark elder gentleman listened to her curiously, arching a brow and shifted his head. With a faint smile he reached over, his hand coming to her chin as he spoke to her in that curious accent of his, "Such a big responsibility for so young a woman. You must feel rather flustered standing in this office, making such an appeal." The man's eyes trailed down over her again, and though the jeans and shirt she wore were not by themselves appealing, the way her body–and bust in particular–filled them so completely was quite tempting.

"There aren't many of us left," she admitted, her tone softening and losing a bit of that customary slang. She was testing him out, seeing what he responded to best, but she had a feeling it didn't matter. It was going to come down to how much he wanted her, regardless of the pretty or ugly words that spilled out of her mouth. "I really need some help."

Kenir's hands were smooth, not the rough hands of Grent or even Jarago, it was pleasant in a way. He stroked from her chin lightly back along her jaw line.

Licking his own dark lips he asked, "These are tough times, madam Alex. It is hard for anyone to get or give help," shifting towards her he sounded a bit sad about the situation. "Most people can only look out for oneself these days. And one's own family."

"Yea, I know," her eyes dipped down. "That's what I'm trying to do. They're all the family I have, really. I just... I kind of got fucked over by some Viles, so I'm a bit at a loss with what I can do. Returning empty handed means they're dead, though. It's not an option."

His hand traced back along her cheek to her hair, brushing along her ear as he felt her blonde locks. "That is a tough situation," he said in his smooth voice, "after the recent raid, it is all I can do to look out for this town." With a sad expression he added, "Which pains me so, as pretty and fair as you are, Alex, I would love to be able to call you one of my own." He had such a persuasive manner about him, his voice quite delectable, no matter what he seemed to be saying.

Even after thinking it over she didn't get it, and the way her eyes squinted made that easy to tell, "One of your own?" She had all but ignored his wandering fingers, letting them caress her unblemished skin and her soft hair, but as he seemed unable and unwilling to help her, she took a small step back. Not entirely out of his reach, there was a bit of distance between them.

"Will you think about it?"

"Well, as I said, my hands are a bit tied..." he shrugged helplessly. "I can give you two options, darling Alex," and he held up two digits demonstrating thus, smiling like a kindly father at her.

"Well, that's more options than I had before," she gave him a disarming look that seemed part teasing, part sultry before it quickly fell away, as if it had never been there in the first place. It was just enough time to illicit excitement, then make him wonder if it was real.

With a soft chuckle he explained, "Just this morning, a few hours ago, I hired a man to take care of our little supply problem," he said. "Hopefully, in time, he will find out what the Viles did with our precious supplies, and if so," he shrugged, "then we will be open for business again. You can wait for that, or maybe go yourself, see if you can find information or something that might help the cause."

Holding up the second finger, "Two, darling Alex," and he stood up, standing before her and smiling down dashingly, "this town needs a strong leadership. My family has done that, but since the raid, I'm afraid," he sighed, "I no longer have a woman to give me the children I need to carry on my legacy," and his smooth, chocolaty hand reached out, brushing against her bare arm.

She held back her laughter, though it was hard to find a way to keep the grin from her face. When the first part finally dawned on her, however – the part where he obviously lost his concubine – she was stricken by both anger and sorrow; anger at how disposable she was, and sorrow that she was lost.

She wasn't a monster, not by a long shot, and each death rattled through her and quickly her smarmy humour was lost to one of mourning, "I'm sorry for that, sir," she murmured. "Still, I'm not... the settle down and raise kids type. Not now."

With only the briefest moments of grief in honour of the mention of his fallen concubine, he slid his smooth touch up her arm and brushed the blonde hair from her neck, "Oh, dear girl," he began, "you will not have to raise them." He leaned down towards her face, smiling so handsomely despite his smarm, "Leave that for others, hm? You would only need concern yourself with the... more glamorous and pleasing parts," and he slid in nearer to her.

"From what I can tell, childbirth isn't exactly a walk in the park," she looked at him sceptically, as if realizing just how sexist he was being. She could feel their breath meet between them, both so close, but she didn't pull away.

The man's other hand took hers, holding it lightly as he tilted his head to the side and approached her, looking as if he were going to kiss her at any moment. "Oh darling, I am a doctor. I have access to medications. The finest for my family; only the finest. You would be in bliss, rather than agony, I assure you. And," he shrugged casually, smiling unevenly, "not only during childbirth too, if you wish it."

Well, that much was tempting, but she still shook her head. "I got a family of my own. Didn't birth them, but they still need me to take care of them. Especially now. Sorry," she shrugged her shoulders.

"If I find someone as hot as me, though, I'll point her your way."

Furrowing his smooth brow he looked disappointed and saddened, "I think we both know that is not going to happen, darling Alex." He gave a light smile, "All the same, if you change your mind, my offer stands." He turned and took a piece of paper from his desk, jotting a note down then folding it and putting it into an envelope before handing it to her. "If you change your mind, just use this to get back in and see me."

With a cheeky grin he leaned in and whispered, "You and I would make some very pretty children, I think."

"Kind of impossible not to," she folded the envelope and stuffed it in her pocket with the rest of her credits, giving him a soft stare. "Look, if there's anything you think of that you can do, I'm probably going to be around for a while. Seeds, food, whatever... But otherwise, thanks. Who was it taking out the Viles?"

With a simple smile he said, "A mercenary. Ah, you can ask my secretary for the name if you wish," he feigned ignorance at the man's name.

Giving her another look over he added, "In the meantime, while we sort out our problems, you could do yourself a favour and spend some time with me, you know? It's no use to waste your time fretting about something you can't influence when you could be working on a future of some kind." The old man was persistent at least.

She really did feel a bit bad, and a lot angry, at the man, and squeezed his hand, "Until they're fed, I don't think there's anything in the world that can shut my worry up. Thanks so much for everything, though," she took a step back, patting her pocket. "I know how to get in if I need to see you again."

Looking displeased with her refusal he bowed his head and went to the door, opening it for her, "Good luck, madam. You know where to go if you decide you truly need something bad enough."

"I do," she gave him one last look before ducking out the door, scurrying to put distance between the two of them. She felt her heart pounding in her chest as she tried to get some fresh air.

Having left the sleazy old man behind, she exited into the light of day. It was already mid-afternoon according to her forearm display, having spent most of her time dealing with merchants, Jarago and then that old pervert.

She almost felt like she needed another bath, but instead she headed right towards the bar Grent stayed at, feeling the burn of anger and embarrassment in her cheeks and chest. She needed someone warm and comforting, and helpful.

Entering the bar she found him at his usual booth, a heap of fried wings and some crisp vegetable she wasn't familiar with in a couple of baskets before him. The handsome man saw her coming about the moment she entered and was already placing an order for more food and drink before she could get to him.

With a wipe of his hands upon a towel he stood up and greeted her, moving to embrace her in a casual but tender gesture before she had a chance to do anything else. "I got good news," he said.

Her body, everything, just immediately relaxed. She even felt that anger melt away and be replaced by tender affection, and she moved into the booth next to him, rather than across. Licking her lips, she wondered if she should tell him she already knew, but decided not to rob him of that pleasure, "What's up?"

Smiling at the sight of her sliding in on his side rather than across from him, he put his arm around her and resumed eating. One thing the man did was pack food away. He shoved his basket towards her, "Help yourself, there'll be more here for you shortly," he explained.

"And the news?" He smiled to her lightly, not the smug smile of Jarago or the sleazy look of Kenir, just a pleasant happy smile she knew only meant he was delighted to tell her good news. "Had the meeting with the town leader, like I told you, and... he's hired me to look into what happened to their supplies. A big job. Very big. Once I check out the Vile camp, I'll have authority to put together a group, if the situation warrants it, to go reclaim the stuff."

She shifted closer to him, picking at the food hungrily as they spoke, "Awesome. How long you think it's gonna take? Can I help? I mean, I can spot my bag a mile away, and I'd love to get revenge on that asshole that took it."

Even in the sweet moment between them, she noticed there were eyes upon them. Especially as the serving woman came by and gave her a pointed look. Grent was known here, as she put it, and he was not known–it seemed–to share company. The fact he had his arm around her and was sharing his food seemed something very noteworthy.

Pushing the fresh basket of wings and fried vegetable flakes to her, he took a sip of his drink and pondered. "Hard to say how long," he began, though the furrow in his brow showed he was considering her urgent nature. "I'll go right away though to scout it out, so I don't waste time."

Looking back to her he sized her up, a faint smile forming, "You really feel up to a scouting mission on the Viles' home turf?" He was obviously pleased by her offering, though the seasoned fighter was cautious. "You've had a run in with them, but you've only gotten a glimpse of how horrible they can be, Alex," he warned, not trying to dissuade her, but showing concern.

"We won't be fighting, just checking things out, right? I mean, there might be some fighting, but it's not like we're going to be running in guns blazing. I'm pretty good at that," she said confidently. "Probably better at that than I would be fighting them. Besides, you can fill me in, right? And I'll stay within your line of sight, but I don't want you watching me and not them, alright?" She didn't want him getting hurt because of her. "Won't let our emotions fuck us up, right?" her voice was stern.

Grent's broad face seemed on the verge of breaking out into a wide smile. She could tell he loved the idea of sharing his work with her, at the same time it made him worry.

Leaning over he kissed her forehead, "You're on a timer, right? So we don't have a lot of time to debate this out," he devoured another chicken wing then washed it down as well. "I'm gonna set out in a couple hours." He looked back to her, "You got the stomach for that? Only gonna give us enough time to make sure you're properly outfitted, then we'll be gone for a couple days at least. Through the most dangerous territory around. I can't guarantee your safety. Can't guarantee my own."

"'Course," she agreed. "Just," she paused, her eyes going up to his and staying focused there, "Hey, listen, when I told you about the group that saved me, well, they helped me get here. They said they'd keep me with them and whatever. But I'm going to take off with you and the leader isn't going to like that. I'm going to return their rifle though because I mean... they saved me so whatever, I don't want to part on bad terms. They just can't help me past here."

Soaking in her words, that old, slowly calculating look of his returned. Looking to her rifle he asked, "If you like it, I'll offer to buy it for you. You'll need a gun if you're coming with me, after all." His large hand rubbed over her shoulder and bicep, "I know the gun merchants and caravaneers around here well enough anyhow. Should be able to talk them into a decent price, even now."

"They just made a deal for, I guess, a really good price. So I don't know about that. They... want me along, so..." she admitted a bit bashfully, her face turning red before she shook away the shame. "Fuck, look. It's not like they were going to tote me along for free, so I did what I had to and now I want out. I want to help you."

His brow furrowed, the look on his face one of confusion; a rare sight for the calm man. "Well... you haven't made a contract, right? You can get out of it and come with me? If not, well..." he shrugged, "I'll come with you and offer to buy you out of your commitment. Either way, we don't have a lot of time to waste if we're gonna get on this for your people," he cautioned.

"No contract. They said I can go. I just don't really trust them," she nuzzled her nose against his earlobe. "I just want you to come with me."

With a warm smile he nodded and gave the corner of her lips a kiss, "Of course. We'll make it quick. So eat up! Get some food in you, because we've got a long, hard road ahead. I don't make it easy," he warned with a grin, seemingly lost in his head thinking of the journey ahead as some romantic getaway rather than a deathly urgent mission.

She nodded, "Just let me deal with them but if they look like they're gonna get rough with me, help me out, alright? I barely know these guys and they don't seem the type but... I don't know, I met them before I met you so the standards were different," she complimented him even as she went back to devouring her food.

"So, how do I best kill a vile, huh? Apparently cracking in their nose and groin works."

Grent gave a hearty chuckle to that, apparently finding it amusing and accurate enough not to say anymore on it. Finishing the rest of his food he tidied up his hands, "You'll do just fine with that attitude. And the rest you'll learn along the way. It's a good day's journey from here with the way I'll be takin' us. The safe and sneaky way," he gave her a bit of a wink from the corner of his eyes.

"Alright, boss. I'm all yours," she grinned as she pushed away the remains of her food, feeling that uncomfortable fullness once more. "So... did you happen to find me a jacket? Hate to be caught in the rain like this. Probably a bag... Got my knife and hopefully this rifle. What else?"

Giving her another kiss he got up and pulled his own jacket from the hook, the thing using some sort of camouflage, it fit around him well. "We'll go get you that jacket and supplies once we sort out the business with this gang you got hooked up with," he said, smiling to her. "C'mon, let's go. Lives are hangin' in the balance here."

She scooted out, grabbing the gun, "Fuck, finally. Wish I had been able to track my bag right then and there but no one ever told me what was out here. Not like that, not like them."

CHAPTER 11

Heading back out into the busy afternoon streets, she had to tell him where he was. "Ah, the old caravan station," he replied, knowing the place.

He guided her there without issue, though she saw Bren standing outside by a warehouse section. The man caught sight of her first and waved Jarago out, the two men watching her approach with Grent at her side with some trepidation.

"I got this," she smiled and moved ahead, looking over the two and trying to remain friendly. "Hey," she stopped a few feet, her rifle at her side, "I found this guy. The leader said he was sending him in to find the vile that took my stuff, and I'm going to go with but... I wanted to let you guys know and hopefully buy the gun off you."

Grent looked imposing a couple meters behind her, though Jarago stepped forward undaunted, crossing his arms and looking from that man to her. "We had a deal," he said in a voice that sounded like it was trying to be quiet, but not quiet enough that it couldn't be heard by all those involved.

"You said I could go and that you just hoped I'd stick around. You never paid me anything and I didn't even ask despite the fact that I still put in a day of work. If I stick with you, I'm going to have to wait weeks to maybe make enough and maybe get back soon enough that I'm not going back to a bunker of corpses," she spoke confidently, completely sure of herself.

"Fuck, it's not like you're bad guys, and if I wasn't in a rush I might stick around, but right now I gotta save these people, alright?"

Jarago looked a bit flustered, the dark man appearing as if he were about to snap back with something. Instead though he stepped in closer to her and leaned in. She could hear Grent shift behind her, not liking his proximity to the woman. "But you haven't paid up all the way," he said in a whisper, "sure I said you could go, but you had to please me. And my buddy," he said jerking his head over his shoulder, "you got me. But you still owe him."

At that, Jarago's eyes slipped back over to Grent, it was hard for her to read the expression, but the caravaneer looked almost cocky.

"You said maybe. If he figured it out. Besides, fuck, we'll run into each other again, I'm sure. Once you guys get back in town or whatever," she whispered back. "This is life or death, and I never fucking had to tell you. I'm trying to be good to you, alright?"

Her words didn't mollify the man, instead he looked incensed. "What? You fucked this guy too and now you're not interested in us anymore?" Jarago gave a derisive look, "What the hell did this guy promise you? That he'll storm in like a one-man army and beat 'em all on his lonesome?" He snorted at the absurdity of it.

"No, he said he'd stake it out and see how many people he needed to storm the place. Jarago," she said his name in a very stern manner. "You took me to see the town leader, and he told me I could either become a concubine or talk to this guy. I'm going to save the bunker with or without your blessing."

"Well fine," Jarago threw up his hands, "but you aren't gettin' that gun cheap," he said. Then pointing a finger at Grent he said, "Don't count on her stickin' around after she gets what she wants out of you, buddy. I saved her life and we got it on. In return she fucks me," he declared, having lost all appropriateness as he turned and stormed back to Bren.

Behind her Grent was unmoving, his nostrils flared and his eyes hard. The man looked terrifyingly angry, his gaze looking like it could've cut through Jarago on its own.

She looked to Bren, seeming a bit more apologetic in her gaze to him before her hard eyes went back to Jarago, "I could have kept it, you know. I didn't have to come back here."

The caravan leader's ego was obviously bruised, and as he leaned back against the warehouse wall, his arms folded, he looked defiant.

The silence was interrupted by the clink of a bag of credits being tossed at the man's feet. "Let's go," Grent said, not waiting to discuss the matter any further, instead just turning and leaving. Apparently the heft of the satchel must've been enough to satisfy them, because neither Bren or Jarago uttered any protest.

She trailed after Grent before running to catch up, matching his fast pace rather easily despite their size difference, "Fuck, I'm so glad you were there. And really sorry at the same time."

The large man didn't say much, but he led her on towards the market street again. As they neared a shop he reached over, putting a hand at her shoulder blade, "You'll need a good travel jacket. Something that'll keep you warm at night, but that breaths," he looked down to her. "C'mon, your people don't have a lot of time for more nonsense."

Without delay he took her in to peruse the shops wares.

When they left, only a bit of time had passed. She had been exceptionally quick to put together her survival kit, ensuring they had bandages and water, and her new jacket was far less attractive and far more practical for what they were going to do. She kept taking excuses to touch him, her hand grazing against his as she ordered what she needed, but she wasted no time.

When she got the last of what she needed, he excused himself to get his own things from the inn. When he returned he was looking almost like another man. His hair was tied back in a ponytail, a heavy pack over his shoulders and strapped around his torso, gun at the ready and a serious expression. "We've only got a few more hours of travel left before we'll have to stop," he explained, taking her out of town without delay. "We'll make some time at night, I know the way well enough, and it'll help hide our approach at least."

Her own hair had been tied up and stuffed under a dark green beanie, hiding the long, beautiful tresses and helping to conceal her a bit. Not only that but she purposefully bought a light sweater and the jacket about a size too big, giving her a boyish figure. She'd remembered all too well what the Viles did, and she obviously felt a bit less vulnerable when she didn't look like an attractive young woman. Her own hunting knife was strapped to her hip and her gun was in her hands as she kept pace.

When they were away from town and heading up the light slope of the valley towards, but just eastwards, of their destination he stopped a moment. Resting his gun down he took a look around then turned to her. Resting his hands on her shoulders he bent down on one knee, "Alex, I wanna ask somethin' about back there," he said in his gravelly voice.

She flinched, her eyes staring at him intently, "Go for it."

His look was firm, but a bit troubled as he eyed her. "You know you don't gotta do anything for my help, right? If you spat in my face now and told me it was all just a lie, I'd still go on and do what I said." His brows relaxed, unfurrowing slightly.

"Yea, you proved that," her look softened as she moved towards him. "Look, those guys were selfish assholes. At first I thought you might be like them, but you aren't. I know that."

Nodding to her slowly he said, "When this is done, and we help your folk... I wanna chance at being with you. For good, I mean." Clearing his throat a bit he squeezed her shoulders, "I know it's sudden, but I believe you, and I trust you." The large, collected man seemed to have trouble getting to what he really wanted to say, even she could see that.

She smiled, but her eyes drifted from him as she cleared her throat. "Look. You weren't my first. I said that 'cause I was scared you'd be like him and that maybe if I said it, you'd back off. He didn't, I don't know why I thought it'd work on you if you were like him, but then... you did just what I hoped. You backed off, and were still awesome. I wished it wasn't that ass, and the fact that it was really, really sucks for me."

After just telling her he believed and trusted her, the oddly timed confession seemed to send him for a loop.

With a furrowed brow he looked away, then rose up. Taking one hand away from her, he squeezed her shoulder. "C'mon," he said, his voice soft, or as soft as his hard way of talking ever got, "we're wastin' time here that your people don't got."

At that he took off at his brisk pace again, over the grassy ground towards the ridge that ran along the whole of the valley.

Her stomach churned, but she was exceptionally diligent as she followed him, her eyes cautious no matter where they went, always on the lookout for danger. Still, she stuck close to him and she tried to keep her voice low, "So where you think they're gone to?"

Grent preferred to travel in silence it seemed, which only made sense with the mission they were undertaking, but he answered her in a low voice. "Back to their hive. New Atlantia," he said, pointing off towards the white mass of circular and oval colony buildings that looked so deceptively civilized from this distance. "The only place they'd go."

She nodded, thinking on it before allowing them to continue on in silence, her thoughts roiling. Why was she so hooked on this guy anyways? He was just a guy, and someone twice her age, and it wasn't like she hadn't had men be nice to her before. Marim was always nice to her. But Grent... She wondered if she was falling for him too.

Still, she tried to push the thoughts away, focusing instead on what mattered - her people. Finding her stuff. Saving them.

They made a fast pace, but the route Grent took them in definitely slowed them for this portion, taking them almost as much away from their target as towards it. Though as night fell and she found herself having to adjust to the moonlight for travel, the path only got worse. Rocks started to litter the way, hindering progress forward.

Her sneakers helped her find them, though she kept scuffing her toes more loudly than she had during the day, and she kept having to mentally curse herself to remain silent. Fear was rising in her and she became less certain of her own abilities, her eyes glancing around more desperately.

Looking back to her and noticing her issues, Grent cautioned, "Step careful, but don't scuff. Scuffing leaves an obvious trail." With a deep intake of breath he offered, "And on the Viles..." returning to the topic from their lunch, "if you gotta fight ' em, they go down like anyone. Shoot 'em from a distance, go for the torso." He was in instruction mode now, his voice filling the quiet night air. "Unless you're an excellent shot, goin' for the head is a waste. They don't stand still. And once they're up in your face, you're better off hittin' 'em with your gun than takin' a shot."

She nodded, her steps growing wider and longer, apparently learning quickly. "Thanks," she whispered.

The lessons continued on for another couple hours before the veteran mercenary came to a halt beneath a small overhang. Moving in she could see it made an excellent spot to avoid being seen, but would allow them to see down the slope at anyone coming. "The sunrise'll hit us first thing in the morning to wake us up," he explained, unclasping his backpack and settling in.

She didn't want to admit it, but she was exhausted. The constant walking, on top of her fear, was agony. She wanted to feel safe out here with him, but she knew she couldn't – and shouldn't. She was even starting to understand how he could eat so much as she let her own backpack down gingerly. "So I guess you've done this a lot, huh?"

Down on one knee he began unpacking. Removing a thick sleeping bag he nodded to her, "All the time," he said. The ground beneath the overhang was soft and comfortable, and the bag unrolled smoothly before he then took out some food. "Spend more time out here than in towns," he added.

"Like it?" she asked, seeming quite curious, if not affectionate. She was so close to him as she unpacked her own things, looking at the food ravenously, "I mean. You seemed at home there."

The sleeping bag was large, big enough for two of them, and he sat back on it opening a plastic bag full of dried meats and vegetables. Reaching over to her, he put a hand on her waist and pulled her in to him. "I only feel at home out here," he said huskily in response.

It was a strange thing. When he pulled her in, it was as though he could feel the tension in her muscles dissolve, and she pushed back against him so eagerly, her arms wrapping around him as she plucked out a dried vegetable, "I'm so fucking hungry."

Rubbing his hand over her side he began to eat as well. It was a hefty sized sack, but the dried nature required him to eat slower than normal. "You and me both," he responded, his back to the smooth stone of the cliff behind him.

"You're not pissed, are you?" she asked curiously, though she couldn't bare looking at him. The difference in their age seemed so much grander at that question, but she felt so needy for that sweet, tender man she'd known only a few hours ago.

Kissing the top of her head he rubbed her side. It took him a while to answer. "I'm sorry you had to sell yourself to that jackass," he said at last. "I don't like bein' lied to. Not at all. And I normally don't forgive it, but..." he hesitated, looking down at her in the dim, moonlit night, "You're a young woman. And you only recently had to give it up. And it was probably somethin' you'd rather forget. I understand how shitty that was. Or I try to."

She rested her head against his arm, feeling very low, but her hand felt along his knee as she continued eating. Even through her self-pity, she couldn't stave off the hunger. "I didn't want to keep lying to you. Not after you said that stuff," she nuzzled her nose along his bicep, her dark eyes glancing up at him sheepishly. "I'm going to pretend it was you anyways."

He paused, something about that last statement touching him deeply it seemed.

Reaching over, he wrapped both arms around her, hugging her firmly. He kept her in that position long before breaking to let her eat some more, a smile on the man's broad face.

She eagerly went back to the food, cutting her mouth just a little in her hurry before finally having her fill and resting back against him. "They most active at night or what?"

Resuming eating with her he responded, "Kinda. They got an advantage at night, because they don't always use guns. And they don't care about stumbling around in the dark. Not that they see better than us or anything, they just fuel on chaos it seems. But the morning is the worst time for them typically."

It surprised her and she looked at him curiously, "Why do you think that is?"

Munching on a piece of jerky he took his time before responding, "Stay up all night partyin' and you see how good you are in the morning." With a wry grin he bit off another piece.

She tittered, kissing his arm through his jacket, then moving up to his cheek, "I guess we better be good out here, huh?" she lamented as she backed away once more, settling in at his side.

The two of them done with the travel food, he closed it up and tossed it back into his bag before bringing both arms around her and pulling her against him tight. "We're safe up here," he said, giving her lips a kiss, "I took us this way because it's safest. It's the hardest path, and it don't take you anywhere directly they'd ever wanna go."

"Even if they're being erratic," she asked as she felt her breasts soften against his chest, her head tilted back as she craned up, brushing her lips against his chin, "I like you, but I don't wanna die just for one go of it."

Rubbing her side and giving her lips another tender kiss he smiled, "S'okay then. We don't gotta do nothin' if you're afraid. I'll even keep watch while you sleep for a bit. But don't let the fear get to you.

We're way off their trails, and I've travelled these paths many a time by my lonesome." His voice was deep and soothing, the man obviously wanting her to be calm so she could rest.

The way she licked her lips insinuated she wasn't quite done, and as she shifted from his grasp and lay low on the ground, her hands parting his thighs, it was obvious. "Just keep watch over me," she requested, her fingers both trailing along his inner thighs.

Grent licked his own lips in response to her automatically, his own loins twitching. "You don't have to do that," he reminded her, their eyes accustomed to the dim moon light so he could still make out a faint sight of her, and he was still smitten.

"Shut up, Grent," she teased with good humour as her hand ran along his package, caressing it like some prized possession. "Just make sure we live to the end," her finger found the button on his pants, dragging down the zipper and shifting herself closer to his body.

That beast of a cock he sported bulged beneath the thin layer of black spandex, it wasn't fully engorged yet, but she could see it was well on its way already from her titillation. "Damn right we will," he husked, "I plan to make you fall in love with me when we're done," he said, his thighs wide, brushing the backs of two fingers over her cheek.

She hid her smile against his cock, licking over the tip the moment she unveiled it. Though it was still a tease, it was something different from her prior actions. It was somewhat amazing that she could make it feel completely unique, yet still so exquisite. The new angle helped, of course, as did the risky venue as she began suckling him eagerly.

Grent was good; he kept his quiet and his head up on the watch. With his two arms draped over his knees and her mouth wrapped around that sensational girth of his, she could hear his breathing growing heavier. The swollen tip throbbed and leaked its precum into her mouth as she worked it, the older man obviously straining to hold in his approval of her expert ministrations.

She didn't mind him holding back. This time, she wanted him to, and she kept drawing him closer to the edge before she changed her pace and tempo, letting the sensation subside before teasing him to the top again and again. Her mouth was tired, her lips numb and her jaw sore, yet still she sucked him off. Her hands ran against the inside of his thighs, over and over again as she bobbed, the saliva drooling down and pooling atop his sac.

It was an apology and devotion all in one, and her tongue caressed him affectionately. She pleaded for his full forgiveness, to get past her lie, even if she didn't need to. Even if he didn't understand.

The stoic man cracked eventually with soft little groans, barely loud enough for her to hear as she supped at his loins so closely. With his cock so stone hard and molten hot, she knew it was on the edge. She could pull his release from him at any moment if she chose to, but she'd been teasing him along endlessly instead.

When finally she felt he'd reached the point that was enough, she finally allowed him that sweet, denied release into her warm mouth. Pressing her lips down in her set speed, she could feel the full cock strike against the back of her throat, her mouth held open so wide as she accommodated him.

It wasn't something she often did, taking a man all the way at the very end, but he was special. For her, this time was important.

As big and powerful as he was, he kept nearly completely still, though she was too much for him to be perfect. His hips twitched, that gargantuan cock of his spasmed, and a flood of creamy cum poured into her throat in long, seemingly endless streams. His voice broke the silence of the night with a quiet 'ah' sound, the pleasure too intense for him to deny any vocalization at all as she drained his loins.

When at last she was done, he shifted and pulled her back to his side, pressing her into his chest in a warm embrace.

She was all too eager to be next to him once more, and as she swallowed and rubbed her throat, her arm went around him. "You can sleep first," she murmured, "Probably best you're awake at dawn anyways."

Tucking his girth back into his pants he kissed her lips and held her so close. "Not enough of us for real shifts," he explained, "you get your sleep, then leave the rest to me." Rubbing those two massive hands over her form he kissed her again, the large man so obviously smitten with her. "I won't let a thing happen to you, believe me."

"Y'sure you'd be okay without sleep?" She realized it was silly to argue with him, but still. She was a woman who wanted her sleep - and lots of it - and had trouble fathoming someone willingly going without.

With a broad smile he rested her head against his chest, "Just go to sleep already," his voice was weary and joking but resolute. Maybe it was the fact he was twice the age of most of the men she'd been with, but he always sounded a little more fatigued than most after they had sex.

"Fine, fine," she sighed, crawling into the sleeping bag. "Fuck you're bossy," she teased, but almost immediately sleep grasped her and he could hear her breath become deep and regular.

CHAPTER 12

When she awoke at dawn, Grent was looking alert. However it was that he managed to make it through the night, he'd done it and come out looking better for it.

Pouring some water into a bowl of dehydrated cereal bits he handed it to her with a smile. "Morning love. Hope you're ready for a long trek. We go the rest of the way today."

"Always ready to go the rest of the way with you," she said, though the sweetness of the words were tempered by how grumpy and tired she sounded as she moved to his side, "So you kill a fuck ton of them while I was sleeping?"

Kissing her forehead as she began to eat he looked out over the valley below. Lit up by the rising sun, the mix of green, blue and old world ruins in grey was a sight to behold. "Oh yeah," he responded, "all of 'em. So it'll be clear sailing from here on out."

"Awesome," she nodded, eating her food quickly, "Thanks for that. Saved us a lot of trouble," she joked back, though her tone was dead serious. She seemed so tired, but as the sun began to wash over her, it perked up her skin and eyes.

"You know, we're probably goin' to see something pretty fucked up, aren't we?"

Shaking his head he said, "No." Then looking back to her he added, "No probably about it. If we make it there, it'll be fucked up. I can guarantee it." He gave her a half-hearted, uneven smile. "But don't you worry about that. Eat up, and we'll head out."

Dutifully he began to roll up the sleeping bag, stowing away the few things they had out. "The important thing to remember is: they're not people anymore. Haven't been for a long time."

"No problem, boss," she said, her tone turning a bit stony and hard as she finished her food, clearing everything away quickly and helping him pack, "They took my stuff. They're as good as nothin' to me. They sentenced my friends to death."

CHAPTER 13

They began early even after a late night, but they saw no sign of the Viles nor anyone else for that matter. When they stopped for lunch Grent took out his binoculars and scoped out the valley below. "C'mere," he ushered her over.

Her pulse quickened as she stepped over to him, seeming more cautious and alert almost as soon as he'd said the syllable.

"What's up?" she asked, her tone tense.

Putting the binoculars to her eyes he showed her what lay ahead. In stark contrast to the old ruins of cement and steel that was a pre-apocalyptic human city at the heart of the valley, their destination ahead was white, smooth and rounded. Low round circular buildings and high, ovular towers of unbroken white were what remained of the colony she knew for but a few years as a girl.

From a distance they appeared purely white, but through the binoculars she could see they were marked, painted, with red. Great, freakish depictions of crazed faces or demons, they were terrifying and the colour spoke of blood.

"Notice anything?" he asked her, hands on her shoulders.

"Fuck, makes the decorating at the bunker look good," she said, continuing to stare through the lens, trying to get a decent grasp of good places to hide and retreat, then looking for where they might need to go.

It was just past midday by this point, the morning behind them, and Grent shook his head, "No. Not that. Do you see any movement?"

She didn't. The area seemed still, no signs of anyone or anything moving but the flap of torn fabric here and there.

"Some hell," she said before she moved back, staring at him, "So wait... where the fuck are they?"

Taking the binoculars back from her, the tall ruddy-blonde man peered through again at the destination. Taking his time before answering her he scanned more of the valley below, though it was so large the search seemed fruitless, "I don't know," he said simply. "Out on another raid?" He postulated.

"All of 'em? I mean... that seems pretty fucking organized to me. Man... this creeps me out, not knowing where they are. I feel like they could be right on top of us and we won't even know. At least when we knew where they were - or thought we did - we might only be worried about a scattered couple fallin' upon us..." she stared at him with worry plain on her features.

Looking to her with his serious, unreadable expression he shook his head. "You're worrying for nothing," he stated and tucked his binoculars away, beginning to get ready to head back out. "Like I told you before, there is no reason for anyone to come this way, least of all the Viles. If they are out on a raid, they wouldn't have come this way. Besides," he said, "for our mission, right now at this moment, them being gone is a good thing."

"Just creeps me out," she shivered, looking up at him. "Are we goin' to raid them if they're still gone?"

Pulling his pack back up over him he gave her a curious look, "We're goin' to go in and scout them out, same as before. We'll see the situation once we get there." He clasped his equipment back in place and hefted his large automatic rifle, "Even if they're gone the most the two of us could do is nip a few things."

"Yea. Like my backpack," she said, hope edging out her fear. Everything about her posture changed in a moment, "Even if they are changed, most of what I had was tech. They'd have to have changed a lot to use that, yea?"

Furrowing his brow he looked to her, "You were carrying old world tech?" he asked. This was obviously new information to him, the two having not discussed it before. He went quiet as he forged their path ahead, his pace having picked up yet again from the morning.

"Well... yea. Figured it'd be the best thing to trade for food out here. Why?" she fell in step behind him, struggling a bit to keep up.

Shaking his head he said, "Just doesn't make any sense. They smash that stuff more likely than they'd give it a second look." He fell into an uneasy quiet, his mind obviously whirling with possibilities as they continued on.

She let the silence drag on, her own mind trying to work through the intrigue and coming up short. Still, she couldn't keep her thoughts silent, reeling with the idea that them having her tech could become very troublesome.

"You said they didn't use guns a lot, yea?"

"Right," he said, his gaze focussed ahead not letting the questions disturb his focus. "They know how to use them, though they aren't patient enough to make great shots. However, they stink at taking care of weapons, so they tend to break on them fast. Hence, you don't find many toting guns."

She frowned, her eyes moving over the landscape, looking for any sign of motion. Despite his assurances, she remained cautious of their current surroundings.

So they couldn't be using her stuff to make weapons. Then what? Certainly not trading. She shook her head, "Doesn't make sense," she agreed.

Lost in his own thoughts Grent had no more to add. The pair continued on, and though he stopped routinely to scope out ahead, they continued to see no signs of the Viles before them. They made excellent progress because of it, so they arrived near the edges of the old colony before sunset.

Stopping beside a series of rocky outcroppings he began to remove his backpack. "We'll strip down to the bare essentials from here," then looking to her an expression of concern crossed his face. "Actually, might be best if you wait here, watch the stuff while I go on ahead and check out the site." The older man's gravelly voice was rich with concern for her, she could tell.

She stared at him. Despite the reason for his protest, she could see the wisdom in it. She'd just slow him down and distract him, and he was far more skilled than she. Still, she knew she was far from useless, and her posture straightened, "You check it out, but give me something less nerve wracking than sitting here hoping you're back soon."

The older man paused, obviously nothing coming to him. The notion of her staying behind and watching their things had just been an excuse, he didn't have more. Though after a moment he pulled the binoculars from his pack and offered them to her, "Keep an eye on me and the colony. If you see something I need to be wary of, give a high pitched whistle like a bird call. Can you do that?" he asked.

"Yea, 'course," she nodded, giving him a smile. "Fuck, you know I'd come with if I didn't figure you'd get yourself killed over me, right? If you find my bag, I might just love you too," she teased his emotions, though there was sincerity under the surface.

With an uneven smile that was at once wry and warm he gave her the binoculars and leaned in, kissing her lips. "Remember, bird whistle. Don't go shooting off any guns. Even if trouble breaks out," he warned. "A gun will bring every Vile for miles running after us. They are a last ditch thing we turn to only after we're fucked," he cautioned her as he stood and got ready to go.

She chased after his lips for a second, then nodded, "Yea, alright. I'll see you soon," she tipped the binoculars impishly. "Undressing you mentally. Thinkin' of what I'll do to you once we get back to safety."

The large mercenary couldn't help but grin toothily at her. Shouldering his rifle he took out his long military grade knife and headed out. For a man of such a size and age, it was amazing to see him move so quick and at such a rate while bent low for cover. It was obvious his long life of rigorous hard work in the field had resulted in making him a pinnacle of fitness and ability.

She saw him close the final distance and make his way cautiously around the edge of one of the broken walls that ringed the old colony.

Her pulse was quick, but she pushed that fear aside, instead becoming hard. Taking a final scan around with her naked eyes, she quickly lifted the binoculars, beginning the slow, careful scan.

The whole process took some time, as despite his speed and ability Grent was cautious. He was careful to stay within her field of view, only slipping behind things for brief flickers of time as he passed from one area to another.

Surprisingly quiet, the lair of the Viles proved empty from what they'd seen. Grent gave a wait sign to her, then disappeared out of her view, going inside one of the circular buildings. Time passed. Seconds. Then a minute. When he returned he gave her a thumbs up, and she could see a smile on his face. Her heart skipped a beat; perhaps the news was good!

Still, she remained obedient, giving him a thumbs up in return, even knowing he probably couldn't see it. The moment between them was short, and it caused her to nearly miss the sight occurring behind Grent.

A red flap lifted and from out of it one of the freakishly painted and rage-laced Viles stepped. Almost as soon as he was out though, her lover spun about. He must have heard the thing before it saw him, for the seasoned hunter leapt and was upon him. It all happened so fast, she could barely make it out. The flash of Grent's strawberry-blonde ponytail in the air, the crash of his body into the Viles', then the two of them tumbling into the building he just came out of.

She was some distance away, but no sound carried to her. With the silence of the valley it was eerily quiet. If the Vile had screamed she'd have been able to hear it, wouldn't she? It was hard to say from so far away.

Her heart practically stopped. The more practical concerns for her safety tried to edge into her mind, but she was already moving. Dropping the binoculars around her neck, her ponytail hidden behind her green hat, she clutched onto her rifle. It wasn't the normal way, however. She was holding it like a club and looked ready to use it.

Charging straight on at the building, she arrived nearly in time as another Vile emerged. She had him, with the speed and tenacity of her run she'd be upon him in a second before he had a chance to do a thing. It was all happening so perfectly then just before she could get there, it all went so wrong.

Two Viles, or at least two–she didn't know for sure–came out from the buildings on either side of her. With the speed she was barrelling at and how quickly they caught her, it was hopeless. She toppled to the ground and all was black.

CHAPTER 14

Hours later–was it hours?–she awoke. Her head pounded. No, not her head. It sounded like drums. It was. It was musical, though menacing and almost maniacal, but it was drums. Clear and loud, they boomed in the night air.

Opening her eyes her vision came to, and she could see it was night, and little else. She was in some enclosed space, probably one of the round homes of the smaller variety. The only light was what seeped around the edges of the curtain blocking the entry way, tattered and old as it was.

Before she had a chance to move, however, it was yanked aside. The dark silhouette of a Vile blocked her view, but she could see the light outside was from a series of torches that lined the roadway outside.

Lunging for her it grabbed her long blonde hair and yanked her, forcing her to her feet.

Any struggle was useless, she found herself helplessly shackled. Even standing at the painful yank of her hair was a trial. More than that, she discovered she was naked as she was dragged out into the cool night air, helpless and unarmed.

"Fuck off," she bit out angrily, trying to slap herself free despite the futility of it.

The Vile, unsurprisingly, responded only with an anguished scream as he pulled her along the main roadway. It was red. Painted like the terrifying drawings on the buildings which were illuminated by torchlight. And upon closer inspection now that she was in the city, she could see all those scraps of crimson fabric had the same designs upon them, marked in some gold hue, as if the Viles had their own flag.

Pulling her along, he took her up the main roadway towards a large central building. This seemed to be at the heart of the old colony itself. Perhaps some important bureaucratic facility of old New Atlantia, now looking like a hideous fortress, adorned with sharp jagged spikes of metal and wood all along the outer edges.

Even though her body prickled with pain, she still spat out, "Yea, that's fascinating," in an anguished tone, feeling his hand tugging her along. She didn't even feel any shame at the nudity, though there was a stockpile of fear resting right underneath the anger.

Passing by some of the other buildings she had time to analyze her surroundings. It was mostly the same thing, those hideous freaks and the white of the old buildings smeared with red. Though she saw something that stuck out of it all; a procession of nude men and women, looking not at all like the Viles. They very calmly walked through the street as if oblivious to their nudity and the horror of their surroundings.

Even as a couple of the Viles came up and grabbed one of the women by the hair, yanking her out of the procession and forcing her down to her knees, none of them reacted. The victim didn't even scream as the disgusting former-human forced his hard cock upon her, rutting her in the street like an animal. Instead, the woman took it upon hands and knees with such placidity, her face contorting, but only barely, as she was fucked before all.

Passives. It came back to her. The other side of the coin. When some turned to Viles, others became the shells of humans known as Passives. Amenable to anything asked, obedient to a fault.

Well she certainly wasn't passive. Even in her quieter study of her surroundings, she was anything but passive. Every step that the Vile made her take was hard won, though it was barely a battle. Not as she was, naked and exposed, stripped of her weapons. She was trying to calculate her next move, yet found it almost impossible to think through the blinding pain and anger.

She could see a few others of the raging monsters outside the main building that seemed to be her destination, though they only looked at her and cried their outrage in wordless menace, allowing her and her captor to push on through unmolested. Upon entering the great dome-like structure she was struck by the strangeness of it.

Like outside, the line of torches continued up the main walkway. The chamber was mostly empty, except at its center. There, amidst a great ring of red flags, sharp pikes and the grotesque collection of human skulls, sat some great monstrous throne.

It was illuminated, though not only by torchlight. Above she could see a great circular opening that must have once been a window to the stars, though now only jagged shards remained. Instead, moonlight poured down upon the sight before her. A collection of chained people, nude as she was, whimpering or unconscious around the over-sized throne.

Last of all was the freakish man who sat amidst that grotesque display. Massive, the man was even bigger than Grent. Bulging muscles all over, he was ripped, probably outdoing even Bren from the caravan. Unlike the other two men though, he was hairless. His head bald, freakish tattoos all over him.

She couldn't help but notice one thing in particular about him before being dumped before the raised platform: he wasn't that sickly, inhuman pale colour the rest of the Viles were.

For some reason her mind skipped past the muscled men in her past and went right to a more suitable comparison in her mind. The doctor. Her eyes narrowed at the man, defiant even in spite of the odds against her, "What, so you lead these assholes I guess?"

The Vile that dragged her in punched her in the back of the head, her vision blanked out and the world went fuzzy. She could swear for a moment she heard a familiar voice, as if Marim were calling to her from the past. When things cleared, the large man was out of his throne and halfway down the stairway, but a dozen meters from her.

He wore little, nothing but two bands around his wrists and a torn and tattered garment that dangled from his waist that did little to cover him. The frail captives at his throne were cowering as the imposing man loomed near enough for her to see the freakish lines of intimidating tattoos that formed bizarre almost lightning-like markings, leading from his arms across his shoulders down his torso.

"Ow," she groaned, glaring up at the Vile that hit her. Fuck, she figured of all people they'd appreciate some aggression. Still, her eyes quickly went back to the more imposing man. She didn't know enough yet to cower; she wasn't yet beaten or undone, and she straightened herself to the best of her abilities, though the dizziness was an issue.

"Can you tell this guy to fuck off, sir?" she stared the leader in the eyes.

The Vile was already leaving, her moment of lapsed awareness causing her to already miss out on its dismissal. Standing there in quiet as the raging beast left, something occurred to her: the people at the throne were chained, similar to her. The Passives outside didn't need that kind of restraint. She'd seen ample proof of that for herself when one savagely took a Passive, never even managing to wipe the placid look of contentment from her.

The well-tanned man approached her further, and she could feel the tremor of his steps through the hard floor.

Fuck, she was not going to be this guy's concubine. Her eyes were hard, but she could feel the fear winning out against anger as she realized just how large he was, and her throat suddenly felt very dry. Licking over her lips, she almost went to take a step back before forcing herself to remain still.

When he was nearly upon her she could smell the man strongly. It was the musk of raw masculinity, sex and blood. His smooth body showed no signs of hair, and despite his own near nudity he had a sheen of perspiration that left his bulging pecs, abs and biceps gleaming in the heat of the torchlight.

Towering over her, she saw his face. Rather, she saw through the freakish tattoos to the face beneath. It was impossible to tell his age, but though scarred, he bore a powerful jaw and a handsome face beneath his stern expression. More than that, he looked somehow familiar.

Her reverie was shaken when he spoke, a deep voice that boomed out but was strangely refined, "You're new to the world," he stated rather than asked. Though the silence suggested he expected some response.

"Not... really," she said, her rage subsiding for just a second before resurfacing. "Would hate to intrude on your party though. Just... let me go and I'll just..." even to her it sounded unconvincing and she quickly shut herself up.

When he reached out a hand and smoothly took hold over her jaw, she had to marvel at the size of that mitt. It dwarfed even Grent's giant paw. "What's your name?" he asked in that smooth, yet loud, voice of his.

One of her eyes squinted in suspicion, "Alex." She quavered with a mixture of fear and confusion, and her gaze darted back to his slaves.

The large man blocked her view of most of them, and she could only make out one cowering woman who seemed happy for the distraction.

"What's your full name?" he insisted in that same steady, loud tone. Curiously, the man's hands, though so large, and obviously so strong, didn't hold the same hard calluses' of Grent's. His digits were tough, but undoubtedly smooth to the touch as he slowly turned her head, as if eying a sculpture rather than a person's face.

She groaned just a bit, though didn't resist his strange touch. "Alexandra Wright," she sighed. She was trying not to talk too much, tremors of fear rushing up and down her spine, and she could smell him so close to her. She was afraid at any moment something terrible would happen. Was happening.

The response wasn't one she had expected. A curious expression passed over the massive man's face, a sort of knowing look. She recognized that look from other men; he knew something she didn't. "From Bunker Omega," he intoned in a quiet, low voice.

Her face screwed up, "What, so you've been taking all my friends? Fuck man, people are dyin' 'cause they–" she stopped herself, physically biting down on her lower lip. Her face burned hot beneath her pale skin and her dark eyes moved away. "Yes, yea, that's me."

The large man gave a low, hearty chuckle though never released her jaw. "Come with me," he said at last turning and indicating towards a side passage. "I have more interesting things to share with you than await those here," he said, implying the captives around his throne as he began to lead her away.

"Fantastic," she muttered under her breath. Upgraded from throne concubine to something new and reserved for a select few. The fear made her skin crawl and her gallows humour erupt into several snide, sarcastic, and thankfully unspoken comments.

Pushing through the curtain that separated the entrance, he took her up a long spiral staircase. Oval shaped windows showed her the valley outside as they climbed higher.

Seeing the trouble she had, he stopped and bent down. She couldn't make out what exactly he did, but with a snap the metal restraints came away and he asked, "Better?" before continuing on up.

"Yea, surprisingly it's easier to walk when you're not physically restrained," she sighed, the words barely even audible before she spoke up, "Yea, thanks!" It was forced, but still she followed, looking around. "So you seen my buddy Grent?"

The unknown man furrowed his brow and looked down at her, "Grent?" Leading her up and up he took her at last to a doorway that opened to a large balcony with a spacious sofa, a table and some chairs. "Describe for me this Grent, and how I would know him," he said.

"I was coming to gallantly save his life when some asshole clocked me out. Big guy. Blondish red hair," she looked over the room, then back to the other man. Somehow being several levels above the exit was more comforting to her than being treated like one of the other captured humans, though not by much.

The look he gave her before gesturing her to the couch said it all: he didn't know who she was talking about. If Grent were captured or killed, the Viles hadn't informed him. Assuming they could inform him, of course.

"I will check into that later," he said in that same cultured voice that so did not befit the looks of the fearsome man. "How long have you been out?" he asked.

She just stared at him, her eyes narrowing a bit, "Uh... I was hoping you'd be able to tell me. Long enough to be stripped and chained. How long's it take one of them to do that?"

With another one of his booming chuckles he rested a hand upon her shoulder, pressing down upon her and making sit upon the couch. "I meant, out of the bunker," he said with a toothy smile.

She made a small sound of annoyed protest, finding the act of sitting bare against the couch to be unpleasant and she gave it a sceptical look over. "Guess it's useless to ask if it's clean."

Returning her eyes to him, she took in a deep breath and gave a bright smile that did not match the situation, "I came out a couple days ago to save my bunker from death. Then one of your little minions stole my trade goods. I would like it back, please."

Seating his large bulk down on the table before her, his legs parted wide, the shredded garment that passed for his kilt did nothing to hide the thick cock between his thighs, nor the heavy pair of balls they rested upon. Shameless as before he just looked to her, leaning his hands on his knees. "You and I have much in common," he stated in his cultured yet booming voice.

"Yea," she murmured, her eyes avoiding his form, "Both our junk is on display." She couldn't help it. Fear just made her more and more sarcastic, and it just kept building. "I guess you have something else in mind, though, considering everyone's junk is on parade here."

With another hearty chuckle he reached out, violating her personal space as he touched one of his thick digits to between her inner thighs, "Yours is cuter," he said.

She jerked her leg away, clamping her thighs closed as she glared at him. There was scrutiny there, shielded by her anger.

"But no, more than that," he continued, smiling toothily at her still. Unlike most of the Viles she'd seen thus far, he was missing none of his teeth and showed no signs of damage to them. They were as healthy and white as hers. "We both come from

Bunker Omega, and are now free in the world. Though," he gestured to her, "you came so late."

It took her a long few moments before she finally spoke., "You're going to have to start at the beginning. I don't follow."

Arching one of his hairless brows at her, he shrugged and continued. "I lived there for much of my life," he explained. "When the bunkers inhabitants went to the surface to start their colonization, they left me behind. Locked up. Not to see the surface world." With a chuckle he added, "But then when they ruined paradise," he gestured down to the devastated colony below them, inhabited by his own Viles, "and retreated back to the bunkers... I was cast out. Funny, no?"

"I don't know. I kind of feel like there might be more to this. Besides, almost anyone your age is dead now, so congratulations, you win this round." Her brown eyes were locked to him, growing bolder without his rebuffs for her behaviour.

Returning her gaze he seemed to grin wider. Her words pleased him, rather than earned his rebuke. "Exactly," he said, "I win." Lifting himself up off the table, he sat down on the couch, and before she could shuffle away the man's immense mass caused her to sink towards him, and he put his arm about her onto her shoulder.

"You are afraid, I understand. You saw the ones below," he gave a shrug. "I won't lie. I get no pleasure from fucking the mindless ones. None at all," he smiled to her, "they don't scream. Or protest. And I like that. But," he said, dragging out the moment, "if that was what I wished for you, I'd have done it already. Your first awakening would've been to me," and he touched her thigh again, "claiming you like you never imagined a man could or would."

A cold chill traveled her spine and she could feel her mouth begin to water in that strange way it does just before vomiting. Even swallowing it back made her feel ill, yet she didn't try to move away, though her legs did clamp shut once more. Her eyes darted around the balcony, scheming before resting back on him.

There was nothing there, nothing to turn to her advantage. Except, that is, what lay on him. Strapped to one of his powerful caves was a long knife, sheathed and held in place against his darkly tanned skin.

"Thanks for that." She inhaled sharply, "So you have super special plans for me, then. And they'd be?" Alex was not good at subtle conversations.

Rubbing his hand against her shoulder he said, "Maybe. Like I said, we have much in common. But first– are you thirsty?" Before awaiting an answer he barked out, "Wine!" Though she had no clue to whom he might be calling to.

"I have something for you," he said with a smile, "a gift. And if you accept it, and like it, you can keep it, and we will get along in time, I think." He reminded her of Adagios' leader alright, though strangely, as bizarre and fake as the man looked with his tribal appearance and cultured voice, his words didn't seem false. "Have you ever wondered why we all live like this? What happened to make you have to flee back into the bunker after? Nobody ever told you, I suspect."

She swallowed, that feeling of saliva warm and pungent in her mouth was turning her stomach, and she agreed to the wine. If he wanted to knock her out, there were surely quicker and cheaper ways. Her arms folded beneath her firm chest, and she stared at him evenly, "What type of gift? I could really use my bag, and if you found that, yea, we'd be getting along. And no. No one ever did."

Before his answers came the curtain pulled back. The most curious sight she'd ever seen appeared before her. Marim. Shuffling out onto the balcony, the handsome, slender man, no taller than her, was nude and carrying a tray with wine and plastic goblets. His eyes were wide at seeing her, and he muttered breathlessly, "Alex."

"My gift," the large man butted into the moment, smiling confidently as he gestured to Marim as if he were a thing.

She was on her feet, staring at him, her mouth dropped open. She felt dizzy once more and moved into his arms. Tears were already flowing down her cheeks as she wrapped him in a hug, "Aw fuck," she whimpered. "What happened?" she pulled away, her brown eyes glossy as she stared at him, "They need you back there! I swear, if you got caught because you were trying to find me..."

Marim nearly dropped the tray with her sudden embrace, but managed somehow to turn it aside and avoid doing so. "No, no Alex," he murmured, shutting his eyes and pressing into her arms. "I... I just got here, they, he–" his eyes flicked to the large man sat on the couch, watching. "They came right after you left," he explained, his voice soft as always, though the emotion of the moment strained his ability to talk.

She pulled back, her gaze skirting over his body and her voice dropping to a whisper, "Are you okay? What about everyone else?"

"I'm fine," he said, though the obvious case of him being naked, shackled and captured belied that point. "The others, they..." he swallowed and forced a smile for her, "I made some deals, they'll be... they'll be okay," he said, eyes flickering to the large man, lounging back on the couch, who was still smiling so wide and confidently.

She kept her back turned, her eyes locked on her friend's, "I'll get you out of here, Marim." Turning back to the seated man, her arm folded tight under her breast, "We were just kids when you were outcast or whatever. Fuck, I was like.. eight or nine. I barely even recognize you. Everyone that hurt you is dead or gone."

Even in the midst of the moment, Marim laid down the tray and began to pour up the wine as ordered, though the large man barely spared him a moment's notice.

"I agree," he said, nodding to her words. Turning he lifted a leg off the floor and stretched it out over the couch, sprawling lewdly before her, his manhood rested out for both of them to see as he patted the cushion there for her to sit. "So, would you like to talk about why things are the way they are, and how things might be, if we all work together, hmm?"

She let out a loud sigh, groaning as she sat next to him. Not like she was in much of a place to say no. "Can you give me a quick summary of both?" she asked, though her face remained towards Marim, worry instead of anger keeping the fear at bay. Now she had to protect both of them.

Marim handed the two of them their cups of wine and gave her a soft, hopeful smile, though the large man waved him away thereafter and he dutifully did so without another word. "A pretty boy," he said before taking a sip of the wine and looking her over in her nudity, for the first time, it seemed, taking a chance to really appreciate her sublime beauty. "Prettier still," he remarked. "You like your present though? Did it please you as much as it seemed?"

"It didn't please me at all to know my people are all slaves, considering all the bullshit I've been doing to try to save their lives. But, bright side, I guess they're not eating contaminated food anymore!" Her sarcasm was icy and she quickly drank down her wine.

Nodding to her words he drank down the rest of his glass as well then poured them both up to the top again. "You are a courageous and dedicated woman to do this much for them," he said. "Especially considering you had no good role models for such behaviour. Seeing as how all this hell is the fault of the old colonists," though he spoke seriously, it was hard not to notice his eyes lingering on her generous assets.

She had grown casual and lax, and noticing his gaze, her legs crossed rather primly, "Yea, well," she paused. "Alright, I'm missing something."

A light smirk formed on his face, and she had a hard time missing the twitch of his sizable cock as he enjoyed the sight of her large, exposed tits, and the ladylike way she tried to hide her womanhood. "When the colonists first came up, they wanted a new society, you see. With no more people like me," he took another big mouthful of wine. "People who will obey and do as they are told. Remind you of anyone?" he asked with a brow raised.

"Yea, obviously that worked out well for them. Fuck, isn't that punishment enough? They fucked up and ruined the world or whatever it is they did," she slumped back, her arms moving to try to hide her breasts. His gaze was making her uncomfortable and she squirmed under it.

"So what, you were a rapist murdering psycho or something so they didn't want you around anymore?" Made sense to her.

With a shrug he casually drank more wine, pouring himself up more and topping off hers as well. "Something like that," he said before reclining back and watching her, very obviously stiff now. Though he didn't match Grent in proportion, it was an intimidating thing to have to be near under the circumstances.

"So the old colonists drugged us all. Made the mind slaves you see below, and the 'Viles' as the others call them," he laughed a bit, "and now here I am, in charge of them both," he stated. Her stubborn refusal to soften to him seemed to be souring his mood a little, or perhaps it was the alcohol that was aiding that effect. "Now you still want to help 'your people', do you?"

"Yes. And I'm not all that interested in helping them serve you better to pay penance for our parents being idiots," she stared at him. The adrenaline was rushing through her body and prickling her skin, and she finished off her wine once more. The heat was pleasant, even though she knew she couldn't escape drunk. With Marim here, she wasn't going to risk it.

Downing his own glass he placed it aside with hers and sat up, leaning over and resting his hands on her thigh and shoulders. "I want to rule the world," he said, then broke into a deep chuckle, "well, a nice chunk of it anyhow," he rectified.

"Hence why you've been stealing shit," she mused, staring at him. "If you're going to offer me a position as a concubine, I already turned it down once this week, just so you know."

Squeezing her thigh and touching beneath her chin with the other hand he grinned wider, "Concubine? No," he chuckled. "Princess more like it," he stated. "Far too pretty and special to just be a concubine." With a shake of his smooth bald head he pointed off in the distance to where the valley opened up near the sea, "There are worse things than the Viles in this world, Alexandra. And the people of the valley have no chance to stand against them without being organized, united and strong."

"And you have a way to make people more afraid of whatever else is out there worse than murdering, raping lunatics without thought, reason, or a stitch of clothing?"

Even though she sounded sarcastic, a chill run down her spine. She had only just learned that the Viles existed and even though she took it in stride, the concept of more terrifying beings was something she was unprepared to grapple with.

Nodding slowly to her he said, "Exactly. Much worse. They don't care to leave any of us alive," he said in a dark foreboding voice, and strangely everything he said sounded so honest. There was no disingenuous tone to his voice; he was serious, if repugnant and horny for her, if the throbbing organ between those muscled legs accounted for anything.

"I have already struck deals with the despicable Kenir Feysar of Anagio, and soon that place will be mine," he said, his strong hand gripping her thigh a little tighter, those thick fingers pressing into her soft inner flesh. "In a bit of time, I'll have the whole valley under control."

Tilting her head towards him with his hand on her chin he looked into her dark eyes with his own, so very similar, "Your people could be the first to join me and my merciless army. Be the best treated of all the normal humans like you and I."

She stared down at his hand, her skin prickling hot. She didn't move away this time, though her legs tightened, "You're going to be more clear about your terms. Wait, was I part of your deal with him? Me and Grent?"

His brows furrowed again, and she could see the confusion there before the name registered back in his mind. "Ah," with a chuckle he shook his head, "no. Why? Did that old fool send you to me?" he asked with a toothy grin.

"In a manner of speaking, yea. We.... Grent was supposed to get the stuff taken in the raid. Kenir mentioned it to me." She was so unnerved being around him, and she shifted a little in her seat.

His look of amusement widened and he gave her another look over, especially those large breasts of hers as they were exposed to the cool night air so far above the old colony below. "Silly fool. We had a deal, him and I," he chuckled again, "I could offer you revenge then too. On that wrinkled old bastard. What do you say?"

"You still haven't told me about your plan. Of what'll happen to the people from Omega. Or me, for that matter. I'm not great in the role of a princess, but who knows, to a murdering rapist I might look just swell in the role." Her eyes were hard on him, and she shifted once more under his gaze.

The darkly tanned man laughed, finding only amusement once more it seemed. "We can work out details later. But once the valley is mine, your people could be," he shrugged and looked around, "managers. Leaders. After all, I only have the Viles. And they are almost useless at doing anything but killing and pillaging." Smiling to her he tapped the side of his head, "I need thinkers. And of course, your friends will need someone to guide them." He gestured to her, his hand less than an inch from touching her breast, "You."

Even if she were to flee, there was nowhere to flee to. Still, she stood up, beginning to pace in front of him, "And what type of assurances do I have that the Viles won't go psycho on them, huh?"

He tapped his hard chest, that barrel chest of his making a thud from the motion, "Mine," he said. With a confident smile, he didn't look disingenuous to her at all. "Savaged and dead overlords don't manage an empire well," he observed. "But I want from you a sign you are serious," he stated, leaning forward. "You are unique," he looked her over as she stood there, nude, her wrists still shackled but otherwise free and bare, "but I need to know you are interested in this offer I make you. I do not offer it lightly."

Her eyes were at him, and her lip trembled, "If I say 'no' will you call off the raid and offer protection and hope to my people? Let them go back to the bunker? Save the town from the mysterious other threats?" she thought out loud, breathing a bit harder. "What type of deal did you make with Kenir, huh?"

The large man leaned back into the corner of the couch, looking a bit exasperated by the questions. "My deal with Kenir was a trade of supplies. He is perhaps one of the few others in this valley who knows of the threats I speak of. He refused to join me, but in exchange he offered to set up some of his own people for an ambush, where I could claim supplies to help in the war against the Others."

He looked to her to be genuine, although losing patience for the telling. "However, Kenir is a degenerate. He is corrupt and will only lead his people and the whole valley to its doom. That is why we need to be unified," he stated. With a shrug he said, "If you refuse my offer, I will have to go ahead with my plans as best I can on my own. If you join me, however? You can try to help me come up with a better way to do things."

She stared at him before she moved back to the couch, crossing her legs once more, "Then there needs to be some ground rules, I think."

Looking exasperated still–and like a man not used to being so–he lifted his thick arms and shrugged, "Go on. Try me. But my patience grows thin. I do not make deals with many," he warned.

"Well, you said my people will be the leaders in your little revolution. I'm holding you to that, and I want Marim to be treated well. I don't want any of them raped or killed, and this is in your best interest. If you want these people to follow you, they're going to listen to me, and if they're in constant fear, there's nothing **we** can do about it. Secondly, I want to find out what happened to Grent, to talk to him in private, and I want him treated the same as the Omega's. He's a man you want on your side. He's a man I want on my side," she stared at him, trying to gauge his reaction to her bossiness.

Irritation and annoyance was what she saw, though he waved it off, "I have said most of this already. As for this man you keep mentioning, I do not know of him, but I will have him found if he is here," he stated. "Now," he leaned back forward, looking at her intensely, "are you ready to seal the deal?"

"Why do I have a feeling that you're asking me if I'm going to spread my legs for you?" she asked, her brown eyes boring into his.

A wide smile formed on his face and he reached out to cup her chin, "Because you are a clever girl. Just like your mother."

"Fuck, why would you bring her up now?" she hissed a bit, her eyes downcast. There was still hurt there, residual and usually deeply repressed. "Listen, this shit is complicated and terrifying. And I don't like pain. And I feel like that's what I'm agreeing to here."

Nodding to her he said, "I understand. You have your present from me, and my offer. I will give you a couple hours to think it over. Is that fair?" he asked, the horrifying looking man looking so casual and at ease before her, his ripped body undoubtedly gorgeous if not for the hideous tattoos that marked him so.

"So you're not denying that you're going to hurt me," she asked, and it was almost as if she deflated. All of the rage left her, and it was like looking into a shell. "If you return with good news about Grent..." she trailed off, then bit her lower lip, stilling its quiver.

Waving a hand dismissively he said, "I will not hurt you like that if you do not wish it," he said, apparently having misunderstood her. "I thought you meant the hurt of whatever moral qualms you have," at that he slipped from the sofa and stood, towering back over her. "I have women for that already," he said as he reached out, brushing the backs of his fingers over her blonde hair and smiling, "I will be nice if you wish it. Sweet even. It will be a fun change for me. So let's go," he put his hand around to her shoulder blade, lightly guiding her towards the door.

She took in a breath, her eyes closing for a moment as she was easily led, "So are we safe from your dogs? The people here, I mean. Or is that an offensive term? What should I call the weak and the rage fuelled?"

"Whatever you like," he said, taking her out and across a hallway. The room he led her into was grand, large and with a massive pile of cushions. It wasn't kept in the greatest of condition, but it appeared clean enough, better than most of the old colony. "You are above them once our deal is done," he said, reaching a hand over as he guided her towards the bed, sliding his hard smooth palm over her stomach to cup a breast, "they will be your dogs, as you say."

She swallowed, but even in her fear, her nipple stiffened and he could feel her skin stand at attention. It was unwanted, and she stepped back from him, her eyes boring into his. "So I guess you must have liked mom, huh? Or hated her. Probably both, from the looks of it."

"As you say," he responded, smiling pleasantly. "She could be stubborn like you, but she was a beautiful and sweet woman," he stepped back towards her, the giant man hedging her in against the bed as he reached for her tit again, that powerful hand squeezing her breast so that the stiff nipple pressed into his palm. Looking down to her he said in a husky, lust laden voice, "I am Nazir, by the way."

That same spark of dangerous desire traveled her body, so similar to her experience with Jarago. Her body craved something her mind fought against, and she licked her lower lip quickly, as if uncertain what the motion would wrought from him. "I've never been called sweet."

With a toothy grin that showed immense pleasure at her response, he tugged away the pathetic garment that passed for his kilt, letting it slip to the ground as the heavy thickness of his cock pounced up. Kneading the supple flesh of her large tit in one hand, he brought the other to her hip and guided her back onto the bed, lifting his left–knifeless–knee onto the bed beside her.

Her eyes widened, shocked at his behaviour, though really she shouldn't have been. Her mouth was agape as she felt his body move against hers, "You said I had a few hours."

Sliding his hand from her hip he took hold of one leg, prying her thigh back to expose her slit. Reaching for it he brazenly touched his hard hand, feeling the reluctant dampness there. "You've already decided though," he said with that confident smile, the barbaric man manipulating and contorting her to his will as that thick, virile cock throbbed before her, so full of desire for her. "See?" He lifted his fingers, showing her the glossy tips before tasting them himself.

"That just happens," she protested, but her skin was already feeling so warm. She was trying to block out the faces of the men she knew she'd be disappointing, but they were nagging at her, trying to tell her what to do. To fight, to get away and save herself.

At least, that's what she thought they'd say.

It wasn't much help to her now, as she let her body be manipulated by the older, larger man. Swallowing, she pushed herself back on the bed, "Fuck, this is too much."

Climbing up onto the bed on both knees he pursued her, suckling his fingers clean of her flavour. He brought the other hand to his cock, pumping the thick, beastly thing, his fist brushing against the pale tuft of hair there, so oddly contrasting his darkly tanned skin. As he loomed back over her she could see the glistening precum on its tip, smell the musk of his arousal, "I will be kind and appreciative with you, sweet Alexandra," he said, his heavy voice almost a purr as he took hold of her two thighs again, keeping them wide.

Fuck, it worked before. "I've never gone all the way," she whined, squirming backwards again, "I can do other stuff! I'm good at that!"

It worked, in that he bought it. The gleam in those dark hazel eyes of his attested to it as he bent over her, sliding his thick girth along her slit. "Too perfect," he said, the weight of that thick cock against her quim so pronounced. "This will really prove you mean it then," he said with a lick of his lips, rocking his hips so that the bulbous tip of his manhood positioned itself at her entrance.

She gasped as she felt that familiar, solid heat run against her slick body, and her elbows dug into the mattress. It wasn't that she was aroused, necessarily, but she couldn't say that she was exactly dreading it. The guilt in her stomach kept turning as she was unable to push Grent's fate from her mind, but then, she didn't have a choice. Not really.

She could fight and beg and run, and find herself in worse states. There were worse things than having a thick cock pushed between her legs, and as soon as the thought occurred to her, her mind raced back to her lover and tears welled in the corner of her eyes.

It happened then, and though it was far from the violent rape she feared when heading out into the Viles territory, it wasn't exactly gentle either. Perhaps it was true to his words as he saw it–the abhorrent Nazir; rapist and killer–but his thick cock was pushed into her with a firm thrust so that it banged against her depths without being able to fit the entirety of it inside.

The powerful man gave such a loud, uninhibitedly lewd groan of pleasure at that, palming one of her breasts and squeezing as he ground himself against her. She could feel the weight of his balls resting against her ass and he kissed her lips firmly before tugging back and thrusting again.

She was most surprised by his kiss, and gasped against his mouth, her eyes shutting tightly as she whimpered beneath him. Her breathing was so fast, bringing her breast to his hand and drawing it away as she nearly began to hyperventilate. She shifted beneath him, trying to escape his length, and she felt... sore. It wasn't the same as with the other two, though both had managed to tease and lick her to supreme wetness.

The dampness that only her cunt provided, given the stressful circumstances, was not enough to protect her from the large shaft's tug, and as he began moving, her whimpers grew.

Knowing how he took his other women, it was no surprise he didn't think this odd or peculiar. He merely thrust into her at that hard fast rate his warped mind thought constituted sweet and gentle, kissing her hard and gruffly, the musk of that barbarian all around her.

As the slaps of his sac striking her with each plunge of that thick, weapon of a cock, he slid his other hand along her body and over her arm. She didn't notice his touches at first, then they became a faint tickle as the man activated the implant within her. Her bare arm lit up with a display of commands on her skin as he deactivated the protection that kept her safe from disease and unwanted pregnancy, all without missing a beat of that hard cock into her cunt.

She remained oblivious to his nefarious actions, her face plunging into her arm as she brought it over her face. Her long, wavy hair was wrapped around her face and neck, shielding her slightly from the vision of the powerful man claiming her.

With every thrust her frustrations and rage built; rage at herself for selling it so cheap once more, at her inability to escape. Frustration at how hard she was failing to live up to her own standards, and instead laying beneath a brute considering ruling a valley. All for what?

Atop her, the rutting savage's only response was to thrust harder, that thick, swelling cock throbbing inside her as the slaps slowly subsided with his balls contracting. His end was near, and he was huffing and groaning so loudly. Despite his civil way of speaking, when fucking he sounded every bit the animal he looked.

With a loud roar he buried himself into her, his fingers digging into her large breast so rough as he quaked with his release. Even Jarago felt gentle compared to this man's use of her, his loins emptying themselves with such savage thrusts and twitches, all the while he grunted and amidst the gibberish she heard a "Take it, sweetie."

She felt that bile rise to her throat again and she tried to hold off the tears that scorched her eyes. If there was one thing she didn't want, it was to seem weak in front of this brute. She pushed it all down and swallowed, letting out a final gasp as she felt him bottom out inside her.

It hurt, and she couldn't help that her body squirmed, but she bit down against her scream.

Kissing her lips again, Nazir rubbed a hand over her blonde hair, stroking it in such an odd fashion. With his mouth open, breathing so heavily, he looked every bit the brute. "See," he said in a husky breathless voice at having just reached such heights of pleasure, "nice and gentle for your first time." He kissed her again, harder this time, forcing his tongue into her mouth for a while.

He silenced her no doubt witty response, and could taste the thick saliva that had pooled in her mouth. She tried to swallow it back, but it was difficult with that thick, hot muscle jammed along her tongue. Her breathing was caught in her throat and she struggled to get air through her nose.

It was such a crude and rough kiss, though finally when he broke it he gave his dick another push into her. The beast Nazir didn't seem the cuddling type, but then she didn't know he'd came in her with such cruel intent either. "It'll only get better too," he assured her, and she noticed on his face that familiar look. Despite his size and strength, Nazir was older than her, at least twice her age, like Grent. And the lazy way his eyes remained open hinted at the weariness overcoming him after having his way with her, slowing his responses, dulling his senses.

"I bet," she murmured, still choking for breath as she looked at him. He was so exposed, and she wanted more than anything to take advantage of it. To hurt him. To escape and run for safety, yet to do so she'd have to go through hell, and she wasn't leaving here naked with only a knife, abandoning all her friends, everyone she'd ever been close to, to wither and die.

But as he softened above her, her hand moved to his jaw, running along it. "That really fucking hurt."

With that touch along his jaw and her words he gave her a wide grin, "I know, sweetie," he said. "First time's always do," and he continued to palm and massage her breast, lavishing in the feel of that large, supple mound. "It'll get better though. Daddy promises," he said, his grin widening almost maliciously.

"That's really fucking creepy," she murmured, her eyes narrowing sceptically. "Like... really, why would you say that?"

With a dark chuckle he lunged down, biting one of her breasts and suckling it hard. Tugging on the supple teat he let it snap back before speaking, "Ah, sweetie," he began, his cock having softened in her, but not beyond twitching a bit with some unknown excitement. "Didn't want to spoil the mood beforehand," he said, burying his face into her neck, kissing and suckling at her flesh.

"The fuck," she squirmed, her hands pushing against his chest. Her face was red with anger, and she looked almost as though she was going to choke. Her voice was shrill as she screamed at him, "You're a fucking monster!"

So much stronger than her, he didn't let up. Keeping her pinned beneath him he mashed her breasts against his palm and chest, sucked and bit at her neck before he muttered, "It's okay. It doesn't change anything. Only makes it better," he said with a satisfied groan, taking sick joy in it.

She was so distraught with her rage she almost didn't see it, but over the back of Nazir–her supposed father–crept the slender, familiar form of Marim. Armed with only the bottle of wine, grasped by the handle, the trembling young man crept closer towards them.

"It does fucking too change shit," she screamed, her head nodding almost frantically to Marim. Her face was red and she could feel the bile rising in her throat. Her hands began clawing at the brute of a man, and her nails dug into the leg that didn't contain the weapon, her other reaching more deftly for the blade.

Marim continued without pause, though he never stopped shaking. He was always a crummy fighter. He never fared well in their lessons and training sessions, and except for the excuse for the two to roll around and touch one another, he always hated them at that.

Before he could get there, however, her nimble fingers deftly slipped the long knife from its sheath. He never noticed, he was too wrapped up in his sick revelry, husking disgusting words of assurance mixed with plans of their future incestuous defilements he never sensed it at all.

She could have picked a better angle, but as she slammed the blade into his neck, spattering her in gore, it did the trick. Even though angry tears burned at her, she never let go the knife, twisting it brutally before gasping, as if suddenly realizing what she'd done.

His confession, his sick, brutal use of someone he professed to be his kin had brought something disgusting to the surface of her, and she tried to push herself free of his naked, spent body.

She was a mess of blood and semen–like the man himself was in life and death–but her strength proved true. Fit and capable, she managed to get his sputtering form off her. All his strength and authority did him no good as he clasped for his neck, falling away to die on the floor.

And before her stood Marim. The bottle dropped from his hand, shattering as he stood dumbfounded. Seeing anyone in pain, let alone dying–even this man–was almost too much for the wide-eyed youth, leaving him looking catatonic as she freed herself.

She grabbed the blade, staring down at the dying man, and tears glistened in her eyes. It was almost something sweet, as though she had wanted something more from him before she turned to Marim. "That sick fuck told me he was my father after raping me. He deserves it. Where's everyone else?" she slapped his face to get his attention.

It took a slap to get him out of it, none of her words seeming to have registered with him. Shocked at the strike he looked at her, sputtering, "They-they're down... down below," he said, swallowing heavily. As pretty as he was, he was just as useless in the face of violence, "He's keeping them in a large hall beneath that... that throne room of his," he explained, those emerald eyes wide and panicked as if he saw through her.

"And how do I get there, huh? We gotta move fast. Are there any weapons in this place?" She was all calm composure, her drive shining through as she gave a quick glance over the room.

"There's nothing," he said in that spacey breathless voice of his, still unable to get himself together any more than this as he tried not to stare at the dying body. And looking around her, she saw nothing. Nothing at all. The room barren but for the useless artefacts of old humanity accumulated so haphazardly about the room: pillows and bed sheets.

"Marim, I need you to fucking snap out of it. Our people are holed up in a prison and they need us, you got me? Just fucking... can you get me out of these fucking cuffs?" She couldn't stop cursing. It was the only thing holding her together.

Slowly he trailed his eyes to her shackles. Nodding he said, "Yeah, I saw where he keeps–" then realization dawned on him and he pointed to the bleeding out husk that was her captor. "In his wrist cuff," Marim muttered meekly.

She moved to the body, trying not to look at him as she fumbled for the keys. Her breathing was a bit faster and she kept her newfound knife poised and ready.

They weren't hard to find, merely tucked against him by the pressure of the leather bands about his wrists. Before she could take them away, his powerful grip caught her wrist, and he gave her a wide-eyed pleading gaze as life–and his final words–bubble from him uselessly.

She stared down at him and his last view of this world was a look of apologetic sympathy tinged with anger. Things could have gone so much sweeter between them. Yanking her hand away, she turned her head from him and almost looked like she was wording a prayer before unshackling herself.

Marim had been watching her, so confused and terrified, he didn't seem to understand any of what happened. Weakly he lifted a hand, pointing towards the exit, "I'll... I'll know the way downstairs."

"Awesome. Will we be passing many of the Viles? Listen, if they come up, you just follow my lead, alright? I got this, Marim. I'll get you out of this." She was completely oblivious to the cum running down her legs, the blood smearing her chest and stomach, and the sweat that filmed her body.

Marim wasn't, however, and he had to try not to look at her, because it horrified him so. "I– I don't know," he stammered, the two making their way out and down the hall, though she had to lead the way to get Marim to move at all. "I don't see many in here," he said at last.

"Good," she followed his 'lead', even though she was out in front, "Just tell me where to go, Marim. C'mon, you wanna be a doctor? You're going to have to get used to death. Hopefully not our own..."

As they reached the bottom of the stairwell heading out into the main chamber, everything seemed clear. Making their way across the room, however, the red drapes that constituted the 'door' to the great hall–the once 'throne room'–pushed open. A large and feral looking Vile stalked in, hunched over and looking menacing. He sighted them immediately and throwing back his head he looked ready to let loose a cry that would wake the whole of the colony.

The moment was almost frozen in time, for it had to be to see Grent moving so quickly. The man's arms came around the thing and plunging a knife straight into its heart as he simultaneously covered the thing's mouth, bringing it to a silent end.

Relief washed through her, though at the same time there was a moment of panic. Apparently her plan of just telling the Viles she was their new queen was not going to work. Still, Grent being alive counted for double.

"There are more in the basement. Do you know where our stuff is?" she asked, all business, even as she looked so damned happy to see him.

The older mercenary looked no worse for wear. In fact, he didn't seem changed at all from when she last saw him, except he wasn't toting his rifle at that moment.

With a flicker of his eyes over her he gave a serious nod, "I've scouted out the entire facility," he said firmly coming towards them. "There should be two Viles down there now," and he nodded to her knife then gave her such a reassuring smile, unfazed by her nudity and the gore upon her.

"Guess we'll have enough hands to tote back the supplies after all." His smile was uneven despite his deep, serious voice, able to inject some humour despite the situation.

It was likely one of the reasons she'd grown so fond of him, "Fuck yes we will. Alright, so just two. That's not bad. Wish we had our guns. Marim's useless in these types of situations, but he's a great nurse. Marim, meet Grent," she smiled brightly, her eyes nearly twinkling despite the dire situation. She really did love the man. "You go in first, you're better at this. I'll try not to get knocked out again."

Grent cleaned the blade of his knife on a rag after giving Marim a look over and a nod. "What'd I tell you about guns?" he said, smiling at her with that look of deep affection tinged with admiration. Something told her he had some clue about how she'd navigated her own way this far out of hell though he undoubtedly didn't know the details. "Knives are better," he said, heading off towards the stairs.

"Yea well, still. I like something I can wrap both hands around," she teased, following his procession with the knife held firmly in her hand. Her heart pounded and she pushed her hair from her eyes, adrenaline pumping through her veins.

NOTE FROM THE AUTHORS

Thank you so much for reading and purchasing our story. We hope it made you squirm, and that once you recover, you'll take a look for more of our works available on http://www.jmkeep.com.

Did you enjoy yourself? Take a quick second to leave your opinion on Amazon and Goodreads!

Connect with us:

Website: http://www.jmkeep.com

Twitter: http://www.twitter.com/jmkeep

Facebook: http://www.facebook.com/jmkeep

Get Pussy Cat Club – a dark, contemporary erotica with a sexy stripper and her bouncer lover – for FREE by joining our Newsletter!

At the end of the world, Cassidy found something she never expected. Love. And a man strong and controlling enough to make it meaningful.

The sweet college freshman never even made it to her first day of classes. She never dreamed she'd be trapped in a bunker during the apocalypse, and her parents would not approve of just how quickly she fell for the buff black man, Leon. Yet when he taught her how to serve and please him, she realized just how much she needed a dominant man to take care of her.

An apocalyptic interracial BDSM romance.

Warning: Contains a reluctant young woman falling for an older man outside of her class and race, including m/f consensual sex, oral sex, and BDSM themes including pleasure denial and an introduction to a 24/7 lifestyle.

Bound as the World Burns is now available.

MORE BY J.E. & M. KEEP

Standalone Shorts:
After Office Hours – Blackmail
Pussy Cat Club – Rough Sex
A Night of the Arts – Exhibitionism/Pussy Worship
Hot Desert Daze – Gay M/M Submission
Don't Lie to Me – Infidelity/Cuckolding Fantasy
Wedding Present – Contemporary Interracial Infidelity
The Lost Lagoon – M/F Twincest Romance

Series Shorts:
<u>Anjasa Between Dungeons</u>
Cutting a Deal – Fantasy ménage erotica
Demon's Den –Demon/elf rough sex
Dragon's Lair – Dragon/elf cock worship

<u>Amy's Innocence</u>
Part 1 – Deflowering
Part 2 – Coming of Age

<u>A Naughty School Girl Collection</u>
Tiffany's Detention - School girl / barely legal
Tiffany – Teacher's Pet – May December Domination
Tiffany's Daddy – Reluctant Daddy/Daughter Incest

Erotic Novellas:
Vile Wasteland – Post Apocalyptic Erotic Romance
Outcast – Dark Fantasy / Taboo
Wheel and Deal – Dark Fantasy
A Son's Devotion – Mother/Son Incest
Brought the Stars to You – Sci-fi Romance

Coming Soon:
Novel: Bound as the World Burns – Post apocalyptic
BDSM Erotic Romance
Series Short: Enslaved – Finding Her, Taking Her,
Breaking Her, Saving Her – Mind Control

BIOGRAPHY

J.E. and M. Keep love dirty, filthy, smutty erotica. With a passion for all things sci-fi/fantasy, and a desire to see what characters do when others fade to black, they set out to explore the most sexual, titillating and sometimes terrifying encounters. The plots are contemporary, fantasy, or science fiction, but they all have one thing in common: they're hot.

From dark and taboo smut to coming-of-ages lust, from twisted love stories to tragic tales of self-destructive needs, they explore the fact that not all Ever Afters are happy, and not everyone's idea of happy is the same.

Come explore the limits of erotica and discover new desires from the smutty minds of J.E. & M. Keep. They can be found on their website at http://www.JMKeep.com.